GOODBYE TO
AN OLD FRIEND

GOODBYE TO
AN OLD FRIEND

Brian Freemantle

JONATHAN CAPE
THIRTY BEDFORD SQUARE LONDON

FIRST PUBLISHED 1973
REPRINTED 1973
© 1973 BY BRIAN FREEMANTLE

JONATHAN CAPE LTD
30 BEDFORD SQUARE, LONDON WCI

ISBN 0 224 00785 8

PRINTED AND BOUND IN GREAT BRITAIN
BY RICHARD CLAY (THE CHAUCER PRESS) LTD
BUNGAY, SUFFOLK
PAPER MADE BY JOHN DICKINSON & CO. LTD

Only Maureen knows what I mean by 'friend'.
So this is her book.

Cowards have small possibilities.
Fame is not won through silence
and cowards
                    out of caution
Are at times obliged to show courage.
Thus adders hustle to be hawks:
sensing the way the wind is blowing,
they adapt themselves to courage
just as they had adapted themselves to lies.

> Yevgeny Yevtushenko, 'Cowards
> Have Small Possibilities', 1959.

Chapter One

In everything that Viktor Pavel did, there had to be a formula, a recognizable plan he could follow, and so, a week before the trip, he had prepared a list of articles he intended taking with him.

Now it lay on the bed, alongside the suitcase, which was scruffy and chipped by age and travel, but retained against a replacement because a new one would be cardboard and the one he had was leather.

Pavel had travelled to the West before. He knew the comparisons at airline terminals and the professional assessments of hotel porters. Leather—even battered leather—earned respect. And Pavel had come to enjoy respect.

Against each item on his list was a tick, confirming its place in the suitcase. He made one final, careful check, then folded the list neatly before discarding it in the wastepaper basket. He closed the case, checking each lock and strap, and placed it near the door, then turned back to the room, inscribing its detail in his mind.

The children smiled at him from the double-framed photograph. Georgi had a shy, almost embarrassed look on his face, aware that the army uniform didn't fit properly and that the bagging collar would annoy his meticulous father.

Two thousand miles away, thought Pavel. Two thousand miles from the safety of Moscow, hedged by its missile complex, way down near the Chinese border at Alma Ata, the tension area, the most dangerous place to be. If trouble came it would be there, sweeping across the border. What was it Lin Piao had said? — 'We could fight upon the bodies of three million comrades and still win.' Something like that. Now Lin Piao had gone, but the Chinese attitude remained.

Pavel shuddered. Georgi would be there, if it happened, fear destroying that smile. It wouldn't matter then whether the uniform fitted or not. He picked the frame up, rubbing his thumb across his son's image, wiping away imagined dust.

Valentina, named after her mother, looked self-consciously at him from the adjoining frame, her face plump from the Russian diet, the expression an artificial grimace before the camera lens she had been unable to forget. He recognized the dress, the white starched cuffs, the severe black skirt.

He had been to the academy that day and watched her play, stiff with pride, and accepted the praises of her teachers and bought her champagne in celebration afterwards in the chandeliered dining-room of the Hotel Metropole and almost cried when she had said with the intense, easily bruised sincerity of an eighteen-year-old, 'I'll be as famous as you, one day, Daddy. One day I'll make you proud of me.'

Impulsively he kissed both photographs and then, although it hadn't been on the list and Valentina would miss it that night, he unlocked his case and slipped the picture folder into the protective wrapping of his other suit.

'Only another thirty minutes.'

He turned at his wife's warning. They had been married for nearly thirty years and she knew to be late upset him and made him snap irritably at the chauffeur.

He smiled, recognizing the protection in her voice. Darling Valentina ... too much love ... too much trust. He felt inadequate, unworthy of her devotion and the emotion began building up until he had to squeeze his eyes shut, his hands gripped tightly at his sides as he fought for control. He couldn't afford emotion like that, not for a long time.

'Better hurry,' she prompted.

He began walking to the door, pausing at the glass-fronted cabinet where she had displayed his awards, the meaningless pieces of metal she dusted with so much pride each day, the minor decorations he had forgotten lying like pebbles on a beach, his twice-given Order of Lenin, the certificate of the Hero of the Soviet Union. Rubbish, he thought. Worthless tin rubbish.

He took the case out into the lounge of their apartment, a rambling collection of rooms, where, because of his position and prestige, they lived alone, spared the difficulty of sharing their flat with another family, like other Muscovites.

She stood waiting with his raincoat and held on while he shrugged to get it comfortable, like he always did, a familiar, intimate ritual.

Valentina Pavel was quite short, barely reaching her husband's shoulder, and like many middle-aged Russian women, her figure had begun to overflow into fatness. She wore her greying hair strained back in a bun and very rarely used makeup, only when she had to attend official functions with Viktor. Valentina Pavel liked attending receptions and banquets with her husband. Sometimes, at the end of an evening in which everyone, even the President and the First Secretary and occasionally a foreign ambassador, had stopped to exchange a few words, each showing respect and deference to his genius, she felt blown up with pride, like a balloon. It became their own, special joke that she needed the corset into which she had to force herself to contain her pride, not her figure. Always she made the joke and always they laughed together, like children with a familiar secret.

She was utterly sure of her husband and his love for her and her awareness of the envy of others was her only conceit.

From her husband, Valentina Pavel had only one secret. She wanted to die before him because she knew she could never endure the loneliness of not having him. It was the only selfish thought she had ever had and occasionally she felt guilty about it. But she still hoped it would happen.

She saw the wetness of his eyes now and thought she recognized the reason and was grateful.

'Be careful,' she said.

'Of course.'

'Write.'

'You know I will.'

'Do be careful,' she said again.

He kissed her, unable to reply.

'And ... '

'What?'

'Oh, nothing,' she said.

They were silent for a moment, then she said, 'Come back safely ... '

The pause was heavy, artificial almost.

' ... and quickly.'

The bell rang and Pavel admitted his driver, nodding towards the single case. As the man left, Pavel reached out and stood for several seconds, his hand gripping her arm until his fingers were white, the pressure bruising her.

'My darling,' he said. And then turned away, abruptly, sweeping from the apartment without looking back. He was quite composed by the time he stepped into the black Zil that was drawn up in its reserved place at the kerbside.

They drove northwards parallel with the river, past the secretly gossiping barbushka at their street brooms. Pavel sat gazing out at the city. It had rained during the night and everything looked clean and freshly washed,

12

like a nine o'clock schoolboy. My city, he thought. My home.

The car was recognized as an official one and the other traffic gave way as they swept over the Kammeni Bridge and then on past the Kremlin. Pavel looked back over the Alexander Gardens at the massive government block, high on its hill. 'There is nothing above Moscow except the Kremlin and nothing above the Kremlin except Heaven.' He recalled the proverb he had learned from his father on the farm near Kiev. I haven't heard that for a long time, he thought. Perhaps people didn't say it any more.

The car cleared the city and picked up speed along the tree-lined route to Sheremetyevo airport.

Dymshits, the Jewish aerodynamicist who had not been abroad before, was allotted the seat next to him on the Ilyushin.

'Paris!' the younger man exclaimed as the plane lifted off, nudging Pavel's arm in his excitement. 'How about that? The women, the food. Wine. Aren't you excited?'

Pavel took several moments to reply, as if the answer needed consideration. 'Yes,' he agreed, finally. 'Yes, excited.' There was even further thought. 'And nervous, too.'

But Dymshits was staring from the aircraft and didn't hear him.

Keeping the habit of the past two weeks, Adrian Dodds went immediately to the single window overlooking one of the innumerable, anonymous Whitehall quadrangles, looking for the pigeon with the broken beak.

The window-sill was empty, like an airstrip with no planes. Adrian sighed, disappointed. No one stayed long, not even pigeons.

He turned back into his office and began his day. He

13

arranged his jacket on a hanger, stored it in the cupboard over the tea-making things and then unlocked his desk drawer. From it he took the felt cushion that protected his trousers from becoming shiny and placed it carefully on his seat, then lifted out his tray containing pens, pencils, paper clips and ink and set it in position at the head of the blotter. My Maginot Line, he thought. Behind the tray, I'm safe.

He was a slight, nondescript man, the sort of person that crowds are made of. He had begun losing his hair when he was twenty-one and still at Oxford and now it receded so much that he was almost bald. It worried him and he combed what little there was left forward, like the senators of ancient Rome. He had considered being fitted with a hairpiece, but then realized that his few acquaintances knew he was bald; they would recognize the wig and laugh at him and he preferred baldness to laughter.

Sometimes, on buses and tubes, he tried to identify people with artificial hair. It was his own, secret game and one that no one else knew about. Occasionally the fixation disturbed him.

Adrian Dodds was a man of no hobbies and little personality who always thought of crushing replies long after he had lost arguments in tongue-tied embarrassment. His genuine kindness was nearly always misinterpreted as lack of character, and consequently he was constantly imposed upon. But, because of his kindness, he rarely protested.

He was proud of one thing, his unrivalled ability to perform an unusual job.

Apart from that, he did not respect himself and knew few others did, either. He had thought of suicide on several occasions and even decided on the method. He would use gas because it would be just like going to sleep and there wouldn't be any pain. That was important.

Adrian didn't like pain of any sort, particularly mental pain. That, he felt, was far worse than physical pain, although apart from visits to the dentist and an appendicitis operation when he was seventeen, he had had little experience of physical pain.

He felt he was an expert at the other sort.

Miss Aimes suddenly bustled into the room. Her entry always reminded Adrian of a bird landing for scraps, alert, head to one side, immediately expecting danger. But not a pigeon. Miss Aimes wasn't a pigeon. A sparrow, perhaps.

She was her customary thirty minutes late and as she did every morning, she said, 'Sorry I'm late.'

And as he did every morning, Adrian replied, 'That's all right, Miss Aimes,' and he knew she wasn't sorry and she knew it wasn't all right. They both accepted that she would be late the following morning and that he would not protest.

'Has he come back?' his secretary asked, primping her grey hair into its rigid ruts over her head. Adrian watched her, convinced it was a wig and that she was really bald. A bald sparrow. Very rare. He really would have to curb this mania about baldness. It was almost unhealthy.

'No,' he said.

'Oh.'

'It's been two weeks. I don't think it will. It probably couldn't survive with a broken beak … couldn't get enough food.'

'Probably not.'

Adrian knew she didn't care and despised her for it.

'We'll hear about the report today,' said Miss Aimes.

'Yes,' he said. The reminder was unnecessary. Sir Jocelyn Binns, Permanent Secretary at the Home Office, always took two days to consider final debriefing reports, so today was consultation day. Adrian had worn his other suit, the one with the waistcoat.

'Do you think there's any point in putting out any more biscuit crumbs?' asked Miss Aimes.

It had rained during the night, soaking into a messy smear the chocolate digestive bait.

'No, don't bother.'

Miss Aimes stop-started around the office and Adrian watched, seeking the gap near her hairline that would confirm his suspicion. Perhaps it was an expensive wig, very well made. Her father had been a colonel with the Indian Rifles and had left her some money, so she could afford it.

Her tea was dreadful, like it always was, and as he always did, Adrian said, 'It's very nice. Thank you.'

She smiled, knowing he was lying, and he was glad when the buzzer went, indicating Binns was ready. Adrian put on his jacket, advanced beyond his Maginot Line and left Miss Aimes to her nest and her appalling tea.

The Permanent Secretary was very thin and he stooped, self-consciously trying to reduce his height, even when sitting at his desk. Adrian thought of him as a question mark, a perpetual query. It was a fitting metaphor.

Normally he stuttered, but Adrian had worked with him for fifteen years and in the intimacy of the office, the impediment disappeared.

Adrian had come straight from university with his Triple First in modern languages, an oddity in a department used to oddities, a rare man whose mind could sponge up and retain a foreign tongue with the ease of a child parroting an advertising jingle he has heard only twice.

At first their association had been difficult, both men sheltering behind their permanently erected barriers of shyness, but then each had recognized much of himself in the other, and friendship had replaced the diffidence until there now existed a unique rapport between the permanent civil servant and his assistant.

Adrian still kept a respectful attitude, aware his hesitant relationship with the older man was perhaps the only real friendship he had and frightened of losing it through over-familiarity. Always Sir Jocelyn led and Adrian followed.

Only in their work did the order sometimes change and that was necessary because everything began with Adrian. He and Sir Jocelyn processed every defector to Britain from communist bloc countries, establishing their worth and recommending whether or not they were granted permanent asylum. They had worked as a team for a decade, made only two mistakes and were rated the best there was, even better than anyone in Washington.

'Alexandre Bennovitch,' opened Binns, tapping the folder that Adrian had created and which lay between them on the desk.

'Yes,' said Adrian.

'It's a good report.'

'Thank you.'

'He's important, isn't he?'

'Very,' agreed Adrian. 'He's *the* most important man ever to have come over, in my opinion. And everything he has said checks out. I've had several meetings with our people, comparing what he told me with what they already know. They are amazed. They had no idea the Russians were so advanced, either on Mars probes or multi-head re-entry rockets.'

'No wonder the Soviets are so bloody mad.'

'What about Washington?' asked Adrian.

'The C.I.A. are like dogs on heat,' chuckled Binns. 'We get calls about three times a day.'

'I think Bennovitch will choose to go there eventually,' said Adrian. 'He's reasonably happy here at the moment, but it's just excitement. It'll soon wear off. When he begins to think he'll realize America is the only place for space science, despite their economies.'

'Is he frightened?'

'Very,' said Adrian. 'He's a bumptious man, but he's very aware of his worth. He'll only go out for about fifteen minutes each day and then insists that both men with him are armed.'

'Could we learn everything about the Russians' space plans from talking to him?'

Adrian pondered the question before answering. 'No, I don't think so. He worked as a team … ' He paused, then said, 'There were times when he was talking when I was reminded of the relationship between you and me … ' and Binns smiled.

'There is another man,' continued Adrian, 'Viktor Pavel. He's the navigational expert, basically, but he was the leader, the real genius. We've known his name for some time, principally in connection with his revolutionary new inertia guidance system, which our scientists want very badly. So there are gaps in what Bennovitch tells us. But the technical staff think they can fill most of it in. Even so, it'll take time.'

'How much?'

'Several months, I'm afraid.'

Binns shrugged. 'I don't think that detracts from the catch,' he said. 'We'll learn enough.'

The two men sat for several moments, then Binns said, 'I was surprised that the Russians still sent such a large delegation to the Paris Air Show. There's been such a fuss about Bennovitch that I expected them to cancel their contingent completely.'

'I don't know,' said Adrian, 'since the Americans and the Chinese established their links, the Soviets have been very conscious of "face" and of appearing over-sensitive in the eyes of the rest of the world. To have withdrawn would have created an even bigger surprise than going ahead as if Bennovitch's defection wasn't important.'

'True,' agreed Binns. 'Perhaps I'm overlooking the fact that at this moment only about six people, apart from the Russians, really know how important Bennovitch is.'

The secretary brought in tea and both men instinctively stopped talking until she had left the room.

Adrian drank appreciatively. Binns always got Earl Grey sent in from Fortnum's and his secretary brewed it beautifully. Adrian had tried doing the same, months ago, but Miss Aimes had produced exactly the same taste as she achieved with supermarket tea bags.

'Heard from Anita?' asked Binns.

Adrian started slightly at the mention of his wife's name. Binns had been to the apartment for dinner several times in the beginning, soon after they were married. He'd made no comment when the invitations stopped.

'I had a letter, about a week ago,' he said.

'Oh.'

Binns waited, giving Adrian the opportunity of ending the discussion or continuing it. Grateful for the chance, Adrian went on, 'She wants to see me.'

'A divorce?'

'I think so.'

'Another man?'

'No.'

The denial was immediate, a little too abrupt. Binns said nothing.

After a long pause, Adrian said, 'She appears to have formed some sort of association with another woman.'

Words of civilization, thought Adrian, contemptuously. 'An association with another woman.' Pomposity for the sake of appearance. My wife's gone queer. My wife's gone queer because I'm inadequate.

19

'I'm sorry,' said Binns.

More civilization, thought Adrian.

There was a hesitation, while Adrian searched for a reply. Then he said, 'At least under the new divorce legislation it'll be swept under the carpet and everyone's pride will be saved.'

'Hurt?' asked Binns.

Adrian nodded, without replying.

There was a silence in the room and Binns began regretting that he had raised the subject. The telephone sounded suddenly and both men jumped. Binns sighed, relieved at the escape. The speech impediment registered as soon as Binns picked up the receiver and Adrian sat, feeling sorry for the other man.

Even with the stutter, Binns's end of the conversation was restricted, but Adrian saw his face suddenly tighten. A nervous tic began to vibrate near his left eye, something which only occurred in moments of crisis.

For several moments after replacing the receiver, Binns did not speak.

'What is it?' asked Adrian.

'There's been another defection,' said Binns, and so confused was he that he continued stuttering. 'From the show ... the Paris Air Show ... a man surrendered himself to our embassy there and demanded asylum.'

'What nationality?' asked Adrian and Binns stared at him, as if it were a stupid question.

'Why, Russian, of course.' Then, realizing he alone had the details, he said, 'I'm sorry. It's so incredible ... unbelievable almost ... '

'But who is it?' demanded Adrian, impatiently.

'Viktor Pavel,' replied Binns, quietly.

At the back of the Kremlin complex, away from Red Square and the onion domes of the tourist pictures, three men of an inner committee sat in a windowless room. It was starkly functional, just fifteen chairs for when the full committee sat, grouped around a rectangular table, without note pads. There was no secretary or minute clerk because every word was automatically recorded and transcribed within thirty minutes, for instant reference by the Praesidium or any security division.

Because they were all aware of the recording devices the committee spoke in stilted, carefully considered sentences, with long pauses for mental examination of every phrase, like school children reciting the previous night's homework, the conversation always in a monotone and devoid of any emotion.

'Pavel's gone over,' announced the chairman, Yevgeny Kaganov. The other two nodded, rehearsing their reaction.

'Are the French implicated?' asked the deputy, Igor Minevsky.

'No,' said Kaganov. 'He went straight to the British embassy.'

'We'll have to discipline security,' said the third man, a Ukrainian named Josef Heirar. He smiled to himself, pleased with the safe response.

'Already done,' said Kaganov, briskly. 'Two men were flown home from Paris within two hours of the British leak.'

'Publicly?' queried Heirar.

'Very,' replied the chairman. 'There was a struggle at Orly. One actually tried to escape, pleading for asylum as well. The French were within inches of intervening. The newspapers in the West are full of it.'

Minevsky and Heirar nodded, in unison, as if sharing a secret agreement.

'What about protests?' asked Minevsky.

'Already made,' said the chairman. 'In Paris and London. The British ambassador is being called to our

21

Foreign Ministry, as well. We're also summoning the American ambassador here, secretly, and asking for background pressure to be brought from Washington on the British.'

'It won't do any good … ' began Heirar and then stopped, aware of the indiscretion.

'That's not the point,' snapped Kaganov, immediately. 'And you know it. The Washington protest is important at this stage.'

'Of course,' admitted Heirar, recovering. 'I'd forgotten the point, momentarily.'

It was a bad mistake and the other two stared at him, aware of how it would sound on the recording. Heirar knew, too, and began sweating.

'What now?' asked Minevsky, after sufficient time had elapsed to embarrass the third man completely.

'We wait,' said Kaganov. 'We just sit and wait.'

The three nodded, content, except for Heirar, with the recording.

Chapter Two

'I'm bored.'

Adrian smiled at the immediate greeting from the plump, sparse-haired Russian who sat hunched in the armchair, his glasses reflecting the exhausted sun collapsing over the Sussex Downs.

'Good afternoon,' he began, politely.

'I said I'm bored,' repeated Bennovitch, petulantly. 'Bored and lonely. How much longer am I going to be cooped up in this place?'

Adrian looked with appreciation around the room. The house was a Queen Anne mansion that had been surrendered to pay off the death duties of a duke with no money, and taken over by the Home Office for occasions such as this, housing in complete, guarded safety people whose presence Britain might find an international embarrassment.

'It's a rather nice house,' he offered.

'Bourgeoisie,' dismissed Bennovitch. 'I've answered all the questions. You know everything now. I want to meet your space scientists, your experts ... talk to people who interest me. My mind is going numb here, with only you to talk to.'

Adrian remained smiling, unruffled.

Only when he was debriefing was Adrian completely sure of himself, utterly confident of his control of the interview, his thoughts and questions always comfortably ahead of his subject. Bennovitch was easy to handle. He'd reached that conclusion at their first meeting five weeks before, and enjoyed proving it at every subsequent interview. Like a bell meant food to Pavlov's dogs, praise meant co-operation from the small, almost dwarflike Georgian, whose personality had been warped by the constant privileges and reminders in the Soviet Union of his importance to their space development.

Binns had decided the value of psychology very early in their relationship and insisted that Adrian undergo several courses. Bennovitch, Adrian diagnosed, was a manic depressive. No. He corrected himself, immediately. Not yet. Not quite. But he would be. Perhaps five years, maybe a little longer. All the symptoms were rippling beneath the surface.

The Russian stood up and began prowling the room, the baggy Russian suit he still refused to discard — the need for association with the known past, identified Adrian — flapping around him, the trousers puddling at his ankles.

His fingers, already puffed and swollen from the perpetual nail biting, were constantly to his mouth and Adrian saw he had developed the habit of removing his glasses for needless cleaning, his hands clenched in tight, scouring motions, as if the spectacles had lacked attention for weeks. Like Macbeth, wiping the guilt of defection from his hands, mused Adrian.

Bennovitch slumped in the window-nook, staring out over the barbered lawns towards Petworth, hidden by the woodland that made the house so attractive to the Home Office.

'Warm, isn't it?' suggested Adrian, setting out on a charted course.

'In Georgia, we have better weather.'

Adrian smiled again, ignoring the invitation to pointless disagreement.

'I'd like some more help,' he said, taking the next step.

'I've helped you enough. I'm tired. No more. Finish.' Bennovitch made chopping gestures with his hands to emphasize the finality.

'I thought you worked sixteen hours a day in the final stages of the Soyuz programme.'

'We did,' admitted Bennovitch, swallowing the bait.

'Surely my simple questions can't tire an intellect as developed as yours.'

Bennovitch shrugged, agreeing with the argument. He began cleaning his spectacles.

'Tell me about Pavel,' said Adrian, sure of his catch.

Bennovitch turned back into the room. 'I told you already. We worked together, always. A team, we were ... on Soyuz ... Salyut ... the Mars probe ... '

'Yes, yes, I know,' interrupted Adrian. 'That wasn't what I wanted to know. Were you at his wedding?'

Bennovitch stared at him, analysing the stupidity of the question. 'Of course,' he said, his arrogance mounting. 'I've told you all this. He married Valentina, my sister. I was witness.'

'When was the wedding?'

Bennovitch glared. 'Why?'

'It's important, really.'

'You don't believe me,' Bennovitch suddenly challenged, his basic insecurity erupting. He scurried across the room and stood in front of Adrian. Even sitting, the Englishman was practically face to face with the defector. Sweat bubbled on Bennovitch's face and his hands clenched, convulsively, bellowing open and shut in his anger.

'You think I'm an imposter, a phoney. You're checking me against some information your embassy in Moscow has sent ... '

'Alexandre, stop it,' said Adrian, his voice relaxed and even. 'You know I don't think that. We've accepted you completely. Here.'

He produced the document from his pocket and handed it to the Russian, who took it and frowned down, lips moving to form the words.

Exasperated, he snapped suspiciously, 'What is it? You know I don't read English well.'

'It's official notice from our Home Office that we've granted you asylum. It's being announced today. You can stay here as long as you like.'

Bennovitch smiled up from the paper, his anger evaporating as Adrian had calculated it would.

'Honestly?'

'Believe me,' said Adrian. 'We have no doubt, no doubt at all.'

'Why do you want to know about Viktor then?'

'We're curious,' said Adrian, casually. 'Just curious, that's all.'

'We're friends,' said Bennovitch, reflectively, holding the paper before him as if he were reading from it. 'Viktor was like ... like a father to me, I suppose.'

The cliché came naturally, without any artificiality.

'He's older then?'

'Oh yes,' replied the Russian, immediately. 'He's fifty-nine. His birthday is on the same day as his son's.'

'Georgi?'

Bennovitch nodded. 'He's very worried about the boy. He's in the army, way down on the Chinese front. It's a bad place to be. If a third world war starts, it'll start there.'

'Was it a good wedding?'

Bennovitch seemed almost unaware of the prompting, deep in his reverie.

'Hah!' he exclaimed, slapping his thigh. 'What a wedding! It was cold, even for Moscow, maybe ten degrees below ... '

'It was winter then?'

'Oh yes,' replied Bennovitch, 'December 25th. Valentina is a religious woman, although we don't admit it, of course. She chose the 25th — Christ's birthday.'

'It was cold,' coaxed Adrian.

'Freezing,' picked up the defector. 'And I decided upon some pepper vodka, to warm us up. Have you ever had pepper vodka?'

'No.'

'Nothing like it for a cold day. Anyway, we had one, then another. And then another ... '

The Russian broke up, convulsed by the memory. 'Valentina had to come all the way from the Hall of Weddings, to see where we were. Viktor could hardly stand at the ceremony ... He doesn't drink as a rule and he was swaying like a tree in the wind ... '

Bennovitch's own laughter cut off the story. ' ... We went back to the flat,' he continued, 'Viktor hadn't been given all the honours then and we were all sharing with another family ... the Rogovs ... he passed right out on the bridal bed. He kept everyone awake all night with his snores ... '

He stopped and Adrian joined in the laughter, as if amused by the recollection. He sighed, happily, a man completely content with his job. Why wasn't everything so easy?

'Think you'll miss him?'

'Yes.' Bennovitch stopped laughing, immediately serious. 'Yes.' He repeated the confession, slowly.

He hesitated, searching for an expression. 'I thought about this ... coming across, I mean ... for a long time. Really it was easier for me than it has been for others who decided to defect. I only had Valentina as a family who could suffer and I knew that Viktor's position would protect her ... that no trouble would be caused. But you know, it's Viktor I miss even more than my own sister. He did so much for me ... encouraged me in physics, helped me. Whenever I needed him, Viktor was there.'

He looked directly at Adrian. 'I love that man,' he said, simply.

'Look.' He burrowed into his hip wallet, producing

a picture of a narrow-faced, serious-looking man, the photograph the expressionless sort of image taken for official documents. 'I carry it always,' said Bennovitch.

Adrian took the proffered picture and studied it hard for several moments before returning it.

'Such friendships are rare,' conceded Adrian, who had never known one. He stood up, content with the information, anxious to terminate the interview.

'You'll get your wish soon,' he said. 'Our scientists are fed up with learning of things at second hand, through me. They want to meet you personally. It was to have been next week, but a slight hitch has developed. But it'll be soon, believe me.'

The Russian smiled, holding out the official notification. 'Can I keep this?'

Adrian nodded. Part of the inferiority psychosis or a Russian's respect of officialdom? He shrugged, dismissing the mental question.

'I'd like to see you again this week,' said the Englishman. 'Maybe Thursday. O.K.?'

The Russian laughed. 'I'm not going anywhere.'

'Goodbye,' said Adrian, but the Russian didn't reply. As Adrian left the room, Bennovitch was staring down at the picture, deep in recollection.

Adrian dumped the Supermarket carrier-bag on the partition dividing the kitchen from the dining area and neatly began stacking his purchases for examination.

Halfway through, he decided he'd forgotten the eggs, waited until the bag was empty to confirm it and then stood, helpless and angry. He checked his list and realized he'd omitted to mark them down in the first place and grew angrier.

Fortunately he'd remembered cornflakes. A light breakfast in the morning. It didn't really matter. What did?

He stored the supplies away in cupboards that were still new to him and wandered aimlessly around the unfamiliar rooms, reminding himself as he had for the past month that he didn't like the flat. It was a box, he thought and liked the metaphor, expanding it, a box where he put himself away for the night, for safekeeping and to prevent dust gathering and from which he reappeared in the morning. Nine o'clock. Unlock the boxes. Take out the Adrian Dodds and start the day. Without eggs.

He switched on the rented television set, waited for it to warm up and then punched the selector buttons. 'Panorama', Andy Williams and archaeology in Greece. He turned it off again and completed another tour.

He lit the single-bar electric fire, waited expectantly and then grimaced as the smell of disuse rose up with the heat. Adrian looked at his watch. Eight o'clock. Food suddenly occurred to him and he tried to recall the canteen lunch, consciously having to think to remember tepid beef, thin, like tracing paper and just as tasteless.

He opened the cupboards and examined the tins, like an amateur marksman selecting targets at a weekend funfair. Every shot a winner, calories and nutriment guaranteed, roll up, roll up.

Adrian sighed, closing the door. It would have to be heated and then he'd have to wash up and the whole thing was too much trouble. He was suddenly glad he'd forgotten the eggs. Breakfast wouldn't take so long to clear up, either.

He stared fixedly at the oven, then twisted the taps, experimentally. Gas hissed into the kitchen and then he caught the smell, thick and sweet. But not unpleasant, not like the electric fire. It would be so easy, so very easy.

He snapped the taps shut and went back into the lounge, and sat down on a couch that he'd never encountered in furniture shops, only in cheaply rented flats, with seats that ended halfway along his thighs, so that his legs went numb if he sat too long.

He didn't have a clean shirt. The thought arrived, unprompted, and he shrugged, examining the one he was wearing. Too late to get to the cleaners now to collect his laundry. Miss Aimes would notice. So what? Damn her.

He snorted, despising himself. Any other man would have brought to mind a better oath than 'Damn', like ... like ... He halted the process, aware it would be unnatural and false to conjure another swear-word. Who on earth was he trying to impress with manly thoughts, anyway? Himself?

Suddenly Adrian Dodds, sitting quite alone in a shabby flat in the Bayswater Road, with its smelling fire and uncomfortable couch, began to cry. At first he dragged his hand across his face, embarrassed, and then realized there was no one in front of whom he had to feel ashamed and so he sobbed on, tears edging down his face and adding more marks to the front of the only shirt he had.

So what?

'We've made quite a fuss,' recorded Kaganov.

'Was it wise to threaten the recall of our ambassador in Britain?' queried Heirar.

'Essential,' insisted Minevsky. Then, almost reciting, he went on stiffly. 'Britain has opened its arms to our top space scientists. We've got to make the greatest possible protest.'

He paused and smiled. 'At this stage, anyway.'

The other two joined in his amusement.

'Will we carry it out?' asked Heirar.

Kaganov shrugged. 'I thought we'd explore the idea before the full committee tomorrow. My idea is to recommend his being brought home for consultation. The

Western press would snap at that and say we were making good our threats and we'd still have room to manœuvre him back.'

'That'll be important, later,' said Minevsky.

The other two nodded. Minevsky wondered what it was like in England for Pavel and Bennovitch. No security committees, no K.G.B., no Lubianka prison, no parrot-like propaganda.

He sighed. 'I bet Pavel and Bennovitch are regretting their defection now,' he said, for the silently revolving tapes that would be heard by others later. 'Under detention, ruthlessly interrogated.'

Heirar smiled again, admiring the remark.

'Are we seeking consular access to Pavel?' he asked.

'In two days,' said Kaganov. 'We've gambled on waiting two days, to get the maximum publicity for our protests.'

Minevsky laughed suddenly and the other two looked at him.

'What's so amusing?' asked Kaganov.

'I'm sorry,' apologized the deputy chairman. 'It was just your choice of the word "gamble".'

The other two grinned, sharing the joke.

Chapter Three

The idea occurred to him half an hour after leaving
London, so he pulled into a layby and carefully reversed
the cuffs, trying to cover the embarrassment of yesterday's shirt.

He examined the disguise and nodded, satisfied. Not
bad, certainly under a jacket. No one would notice. Well,
almost no one. Miss Aimes would see it, immediately.
Adrian pictured the quick smirk, the half nod of secret
confirmation. Perhaps her wig would fall off. He wondered
if she washed wigs like shirts ... 'Is your wig whiter than
white? If not, use ... '

He smiled and pulled out into the traffic again. He had
been to the house before and so he was familiar with the
route and his mind butterflied, hovering around the forthcoming interview. A preliminary meeting, Sir Jocelyn
had said. Let's assure ourselves completely that he's the
right man. It wouldn't be difficult, thought Adrian, with
the guidance he'd already got from Bennovitch.

He'd be on his way back by three and that was important because Sir Jocelyn was awaiting his return. The
baronet would probably suggest his club, but Adrian had
already practised the refusal, unwilling to sacrifice the
time.

Anita had stipulated eight o'clock.

Adrian recognized the turn just before Pulborough and
swung in, slowed by the narrowness of the lanes. Like that
in which Bennovitch was hidden, only a few miles away,
the house had once been a country retreat, lying deep in

easily guarded, wooded grounds and now adopted for its specialized purpose, a prison without bars or warders, a place which kept out people instead of detaining them.

Pavel had been brought there the previous night, by a roundabout route from the house in London where he had been kept for the twenty-four hours since his helicopter flight from the NATO headquarters in Brussels. Adrian knew the men whose responsibility it was to keep Pavel alive, but nevertheless went through the regulation procedure of identification, even having his fingerprints taken and matched against the records already at the house of those half dozen people who were to be allowed access, once all other checks had been passed.

The routine was followed without any half cynical 'I'm sorry, but ... ' smiles from the men appointed to guard Pavel. The second Russian defector had been allotted the highest security risk rating, ensuring a permanent guard of twenty men, two in constant attendance except for debriefings, even for lavatory visits.

Pavel was breakfasting when Adrian arrived and the Englishman watched him through one of the observation points fitted into every room. The scientist ate solidly, unconcerned at the security men who sat near the door, silently observing the meal.

Eggs, thought Adrian. Yellow, crisply fried eggs and toast, with the choice of preserves or marmalade. His stomach felt empty and echoed its hollowness with a belch, which he subdued. He turned away from the observation point, embarrassed.

'It's like watching an animal feed, at the zoo,' he said to the man who stood alongside. The security official shrugged. 'Your department fixed the classification,' he said. 'We just do as we're told and hope to Christ nothing goes wrong.'

Adrian didn't reply. He stood in the hallway until the breakfast was cleared and then gave the scientist ten minutes before moving into the room. The Russian looked up, acknowledging a new face.

'Good morning,' said Adrian, smiling, his accent perfect.

Pavel smiled and ducked his head in appreciation. 'I speak English,' he said.

'As you wish,' responded Adrian.

'But I wish my English were as good as your Russian.'

Adrian smiled at the compliment. 'Perhaps I have more practice.'

'Perhaps.'

Adrian half turned to the security men, who rose together. One nodded and said, 'Think we'll take a break.'

He spoke in Russian, too, and Pavel laughed, aloud. 'Perhaps I should start awarding marks.'

Adrian sat in a deep leather armchair bordering the fire, studying the other man, marking the contrasts with Bennovitch. Pavel was medium height, but quite thin, unlike his squat, rotund partner, and the fastidiousness showed. He appeared quite relaxed, hands cupped in his lap, nails clean and well manicured, his suit crisp and pressed and better cut than that of Bennovitch, showing almost Western tailoring. The eyes were blank and unrevealing behind the spectacles, the receding hair separated by a parting that was ruler-straight.

'You must be one of the important men,' said Pavel. 'What would the word be — quizmaster?'

Adrian felt he was being laughed at. He smiled at the irony. Unusual confidence, he thought. Normally there was more uncertainty. He shrugged, adopting the diffident attitude so necessary to question arrogant men who made mistakes because they thought they dominated the interview.

'I wouldn't say that,' he replied. 'I'm just convenient because I speak languages.'

'How many?' asked Pavel, immediately.

34

Unusual again, thought Adrian. He'd used the dismissive ploy several times in the past, but never been challenged on it. As a rule they were nervous, concerned only with questions revolving around their own safety.

'Quite a few,' he said, still modest.

'But how many?' There was an edge of impatience in the query, showing a man used to questions being specifically answered the first time, without prevarication.

'Twelve,' replied Adrian, immediately. Let him dominate the interview, initially, just to gather more confidence.

'Chinese?'

The question was a surprise until Adrian remembered the boy on the Chinese border. 'Mandarin and Cantonese, and one dialect.'

Pavel nodded, as if the answers had solved some secret questions.

'Are you worried about Georgi?' asked Adrian, shifting the initiative.

Pavel smiled. 'Georgi? You know of my son?' Then without awaiting an answer, he said confidently, 'Alexandre has been talking.'

Adrian wondered whether to disclose that the fact had come from the Moscow embassy and decided against it. Let him think Bennovitch was being co-operative.

'He's very fond of you,' said Adrian. 'He refers to you almost as a father.'

Clever, thought Adrian. So far he's effortlessly avoided the only question.

'Is Alexandre happy?'

Adrian shrugged again, still allowing the control to slide away from him.

'Of course not,' he said. 'Any more than you are now or will be for some months yet. There's too much uncertainty and anxiety yet for there to be any enjoyment apart from the exhilaration of getting away.'

35

It had been a tenet of his psychology training to be as honest as possible with any interviewee. The moment the subject caught the questioner in a basic dishonesty, any hope of co-operation disappeared. Pavel nodded, accepting the attitude.

'Does it get better? How long does the uncertainty last?'

Adrian thought he saw a gap in the confidence and moved to widen it.

'It depends on the person,' he said.

'I feel guilty,' admitted Pavel suddenly, and Adrian stepped in, accepting the opening.

'That's inevitable,' he said, 'and it'll be more difficult for you than it was for Alexandre. He only left a sister. And being your wife, she was protected. But now she isn't. Neither are Georgi or Valentina.'

Adrian had spoken purposely, trying to shatter the man's demeanour, accepting the frowns that the abrupt questions and statements would later cause among the people who argued that there should be as few reminders as possible of the difficulties that a defection caused an émigré's family. Pavel was going to be difficult, perhaps the most difficult yet. The reaction is worth the risk, judged Adrian.

'You're not taking any notes,' said Pavel, suddenly.

'No.'

'So everything is being recorded?'

Adrian sighed. It *was* going to be the most difficult.

'Yes,' he said.

'Funny,' mused Pavel. 'I knew it was done in Russia, but I never imagined it being done here ... '

' ... It's for convenience,' broke in Adrian. It was important to establish a guide to this drifting conversation. 'Notebooks or unspeaking shorthand writers in the corner of a room unsettle people, make them aware that every word is being noted. A tape recording is a convenience, that's all. We make no secret of it. I *could* have lied.'

'But that would have been pointless, wouldn't it?' said Pavel. 'And endangered any confidence growing between us.'

Adrian frowned, unsettled by the other man's knowledge. Where had a space scientist learned psychology? Pavel stared around the elegant breakfast room. 'There are observation points, of course.'

Adrian hesitated, momentarily, feeling himself blush. He decided to maintain the honesty and said, 'Of course.'

He paused, then added, 'It's a protection device, for your safety ... '

Pavel's ridicule cut him off.

'Hah! That was a mistake,' snorted Pavel. 'So far you've been honest with me and I've recognized it. But that was stupid. I came to England in the dead of night, by helicopter from the Continent. So no one in the world knows exactly where I am except the people you choose to know. It's not *my* safety you're worried about at the moment.'

Adrian decided he had to jar the other man's confidence.

'For a man who has abandoned his family and his country and knowingly become a traitor, you're remarkably unconcerned,' he said. That question would cause more than frowns. There would be complaints now.

Pavel looked at him, solidly, measuring his reply.

'Are people usually nervous then?'

Adrian refused to let the initiative get away from him. 'Aren't you?' he retorted.

Pavel smiled. 'Yes — very,' he admitted. There was a pause, and then he added, 'And I'm very conscious of what I've done to my family.'

'Then why have you come over?' Adrian maintained the aggression, anxious to establish supremacy.

37

Again Pavel took time to reply and spoke haltingly, uttering the thoughts as they came to him. 'I thought my work was more important to me than anything else ... even before Alexandre defected from the congress in Helsinki. I was getting more and more frustrated at the restrictions that were being imposed upon me ... I'd even thought of trying to get away, not knowing Alexandre was thinking the same way ... '

The Russian smiled, suddenly. 'Alexandre never indicated a thing,' he said. 'I had no idea what he was planning. Me! — He wouldn't even trust me.'

He sounded hurt.

'I know,' said Adrian.

Pavel took up the explanation again. 'With Alexandre gone, our programme was broken. I could have got another colleague, certainly, but it would have taken too long — years — to get to the level at which Alexandre and I were working.'

'Why did the Russians let you go to the air show, so soon after Bennovitch's defection?'

Adrian spaced his question, the most important he had to put initially to the scientist.

Pavel shrugged, accepting the emphasis that the Englishman placed upon it, but dismissing it. 'But whyever shouldn't they?' he said, rhetorically. 'As far as the authorities are concerned, my return was guaranteed ... my wife and daughter in Moscow ... my son at Alma Ata. They thought they had enough hostages to let me take up my exit visa ... '

'But they were wrong?'

Pavel didn't reply. Adrian was quite relaxed now, analysing everything the Russian said.

'You spoke in a strange tense a little while ago,' continued Adrian. 'You said you thought your work was more important than your family, as if you'd changed your mind now. Have you?'

38

Pavel humped his shoulders in uncertainty. 'I don't know,' he said. 'It's just that ... that I don't have the feeling I expected to have. I keep thinking of Valentina ... of the girl ... of what will happen to them ... '

He trailed off, swallowing. Adrian let him recover, knowing the Russian would sense the gesture and appreciate it, perhaps become less hostile.

'See.'

Pavel took a large wallet from inside his jacket, the size making it difficult to get from his pocket.

'My children,' identified the scientist, proudly.

Adrian examined the boy in soldier's uniform and the girl in her stiff graduation dress.

'Georgi is a lieutenant,' said Pavel, the proud father. 'They've let Valentina stay on at the academy. They say she's so good that she could become a concert violinist.'

'Nice children,' said Adrian, inadequately.

'I miss them,' said Pavel, softly, his voice reflective.

'Bennovitch doesn't know you're here yet,' said Adrian, wanting to break the other man's mood. 'He'll be excited. His chief regret is the thought of not seeing you again ... '

Adrian paused, then extended the lure. 'He was reminiscing yesterday, talking of your wedding ... '

He stopped, purposely, and waited. Pavel smiled. 'God, he got me drunk,' he said. And then, in snatches, repeated the story that the other Russian had told, confirming details that it would never have occurred to the Russians to furnish any assassin impostor.

But unlike Bennovitch, the memory saddened Pavel. 'I thought I had let Valentina down then,' he said, disgustedly. 'Now look.'

Adrian glanced at his watch and realized he had been with the Russian for three hours. It surprised him. Pavel saw the move and recovered some of his earlier arrogance.

'Satisfied?' he asked.

'This was only a preliminary meeting...' began Adrian, but the other man completed the sentence: '... to make sure I was genuine.'

'... to make sure you were genuine,' agreed Adrian.

'And am I?'

'I think so.'

'And they'll take your word alone?'

'We'll meet again,' said Adrian and once more the Russian cut in.

'For more recordings to be made and examined for accuracy.'

'... for more recordings to be made and examined for accuracy,' echoed Adrian. 'But ultimately the decision on whether or not you're granted permanent asylum will be made upon my report.'

'I was right,' said Pavel. 'You are one of the important ones.'

'I get the feeling you enjoy being right all the time, don't you Viktor?'

The Russian reacted to the sarcasm, frowning. Adrian wondered whether the response was at the irony or the intentional disrespect of using his christian name.

'Are you often rude?' snapped Pavel.

'Not often,' said Adrian, honestly.

'I don't think you and I are going to establish a relationship,' said the Russian pompously. 'I want someone else to examine me.'

Adrian laughed, the amusement genuine but protracted to arouse the other man's anger.

'But you're not in a position to make demands, Viktor,' he said, carefully stressing the christian name again.

'You want my help,' reminded Pavel, almost triumphantly, like a man laying a winning card in a whist game.

'Not as much as you need ours,' trumped Adrian.

Pavel stood up and walked to the window, speaking with his back to Adrian.

'I expected to be treated differently from this,' he said, but there was an uncertainty in his voice. The confidence was being chipped away.

'Perhaps we both did,' remarked Adrian, mildly, a note of dismissal in his voice.

He stood up and when he spoke again his attitude was one of complete superiority, calculated to annoy the Russian.

'I'll be here again at nine tomorrow morning,' he said, curtly. 'Try and be ready, will you? I had to wait twenty minutes for you today.'

He heard the Russian turn, to reply, but swept out of the room before he had chance to speak, ending the interview on his own terms.

Adrian drove slowly back to London, allowing the motorcycle dispatch-rider ahead of him adequate time to deliver the tape, so that his conversation with Sir Jocelyn would not be a parrot-like recital of facts.

Adrian was uneasy.

The man he had just left was definitely Viktor Pavel, the other half of the most important space scientist team that the Russians had ever established. He was the man in Bennovitch's photograph and the personal account that the man had provided tallied with every detail from the first defector and from the Moscow embassy.

Unquestionably, once the confidence had been eroded, the man would co-operate, filling in the gaps of Bennovitch's debriefing, giving the West the most comprehensive account of the Russians' space development and future planning.

And yet?

Adrian edged through the early afternoon traffic, towards Westminster Bridge, unable to isolate the doubt in his mind. Or remove it.

Binns was waiting for him in his office, characteristically

hunched, his face expressionless. Adrian lowered himself into his usual chair and then remembered his cuffs, lowering his arms uncomfortably by his side. Sir Jocelyn did not appear to notice.

'You heard the tapes?'

Binns nodded.

'And?'

Sir Jocelyn did not reply. 'Others heard them, too,' he said and Adrian detected a curtness in his voice. 'Even the Prime Minister sat in.'

'Well?'

'They thought you handled the interview appallingly.' He slowed, then added, quickly, embarrassed almost, 'So did I.'

Adrian was shocked. He'd realized the way that the interview had gone and anticipated the criticism that his attitude would arouse among some people. But he never expected it to extend to the Permanent Secretary. Sir Jocelyn was his friend. Adrian felt let down.

'You?' he said, the surprise showing.

'Yes,' said Binns and because of the stress, the impediment began to clutter the conversation. The nerve jumped near his eye, the indicator of stress.

' ... antagonized the man ... he's hostile now ... resentful ... won't help ... '

'But that's not true.' Halfway through the protest, Adrian's voice cracked, so that it finished on a whining note.

'Pavel *is* hostile,' said Adrian, coughing. 'For years he's led a favoured life, treated with special respect. I had to handle him like that, don't you see?'

'No,' said Sir Jocelyn stiffly. 'No, I don't. And neither do the others.'

'Then they're stupid,' said Adrian, surprised at his own vehemence, aware he was including Binns in the condemnation.

'I've got to antagonize him, humiliate him, to a degree. If he feels that he is controlling the interview, then it will be pointless and the debriefing will take months. If he's allowed control, real control, not just that which I contrive to allow him, then all we'll learn is what he *wants* us to know, not what *we* want to learn.'

'The Prime Minister wants you taken off the debriefing,' announced Binns, abruptly.

Adrian stared out of the window, following a flock of pigeons, aware that his eyes were misted and that he couldn't see very well. He wondered if the bird with the broken beak were among them.

'I said they want you taken off the Pavel debriefing.'

'I heard,' said Adrian, with difficulty. Then, his voice growing stronger, he said, 'Are you going to suspend me?'

Binns hesitated. 'I don't know,' he said. 'The recordings sounded bad, but considering the explanation you've given, there seems some sense in your attitude. Pavel *was* arrogant.'

'So?'

'The decision was left to me,' said Binns. 'I think you should continue.'

As Adrian slowly released his sigh, the other man added, 'At least for one more meeting.'

'One last chance?' said Adrian, surprised at his own sarcasm.

Binns held out his hands, an expression of helplessness. 'You can't begin to appreciate the pressure of this thing,' he said, apologetically. 'We've got the whole Russian space programme for the next decade, here in our hands. We daren't make the slightest mistake.'

'If you replace me,' said Adrian, desperately, 'then you'll be making just such a mistake. Handle Pavel gently, in the early stages, and you'll get nothing, nothing that he doesn't want you to get.'

43

Binns frowned. 'You're talking as if he's not genuine ... as if he's not serious about defecting ... '

'Oh, he's genuine,' corrected Adrian, immediately. 'I've no doubts at all that he *is* Viktor Pavel.'

'Then what?'

'I don't know,' said Adrian, knowing it sounded inadequate. 'Something is not right.'

'But what? There must be something.'

'His attitude,' said Adrian. 'Didn't it strike you as odd, the way he sounded on the recording?'

Binns smiled, apologetic again. 'Actually,' he said, 'a good deal more attention was devoted to your attitude.'

'Then that was an error,' said Adrian, primly. 'Play it again.'

Binns pressed a button set into a console on his desk and the sounds of that morning's interview echoed round the room. They both sat, unspeaking, for a long time and then Binns stopped the track.

'Well?' he asked.

'He's too confident,' said Adrian. 'Think of it. A top scientist, a man in an honoured position, able to make almost any demand and know it will be met, someone who knows that his defection will cause untold hardships to the wife he adores and the children he idolizes, suddenly decides to turn traitor and cross to the West ... '

'But he explained that,' cut in Binns. 'He's a scientist, a man to whom research is all-important ... '

'He's not,' snapped Adrian, his turn to interrupt. 'Pavel's no white-haired eccentric with his head in the clouds. He's a very clever, very dedicated man. He's the sort of person who never makes a sudden, unconsidered move. And he's not frightened.'

'Frightened?'

'Yes. Frightened,' said Adrian. 'What's the feeling they all have when they come across, the very first thing that

44

registers when you go in for the first time and speak to them? It's nervousness. It's the uncertainty of not knowing what's going to happen to them, the doubt about whether we'll accept them or whether we'll torture them, like their propaganda says we do. If a car backfires they leap eight feet into the air, imagining it's an assassin's bullet. You can smell the fear on them, like sweat. Everyone has it, everyone I've ever debriefed.'

'Except Pavel?'

'Except Pavel,' agreed Adrian. 'Listen to that tape again. He's measuring me, flippantly almost. That man was playing a mental game of chess, a game he was far too confident of winning.'

Binns toyed with a paperweight, arched forward in thought.

'But what's the point?' he asked. 'Just for the sake of argument, let's accept these suspicions of yours. What on earth can it achieve?'

Adrian shook his head, aware of the flaw. 'I don't know,' he admitted. 'I just can't think of an explanation. All I feel is the doubt.'

'I'm not going to get very far with the Prime Minister tomorrow, trying to explain a vague feeling devoid of evidence.'

'I know,' accepted Adrian. 'And I know it makes my attitude look stupid.'

'The Minister will dismiss it as pique because someone got the better of you for the first time in a debriefing.'

'Do you?' jumped in Adrian, quickly, anxious for the answer.

'No,' said Binns, 'no. I don't. I accept completely your explanation for the way you conducted the meeting.'

'But not my surmise?'

'Give me some proof, anything, some lie the man tells. Then I'll try and see it. At the moment, I think we've got a genuine defector who is perhaps covering the nervousness you regard as so important with a great show of confidence.'

He paused. Then, reminding Adrian of the psychology training, he asked, 'Isn't over-confidence one of the surest signs of an inferiority complex?'

Adrian nodded. 'I accept there's nothing you can relay to the P.M.' he said.

The Permanent Secretary glanced at the clock and stood up and then, as Adrian had anticipated, said, 'Why don't we have a drink at my club, to cover the finer points?'

'Do you mind if I don't?' said Adrian, immediately noticing the change in attitude of his chief, the withdrawal of a shy man who has been rejected.

'No,' said Binns, immediately, sitting down again awkwardly. 'No, of course not.'

'I've got to see someone … ' began Adrian, recognizing the emptiness of the statement. He blurted out, 'Anita has asked me to see her.'

Binns's attitude evaporated.

'You'll go down to Pulborough tomorrow?'

'Yes — I expect there'll be some technical questions waiting for me in the office.'

'This time tomorrow then?'

'Yes.'

'And Adrian … '

'What?'

'I know … perhaps I'm the only one who does … how much the breakup of your marriage to Anita means. But remember who you are and what you're doing. What you're involved in at the moment is far more important than your personal life. It's *the* most important thing you're ever likely to get involved in and that's a sweeping statement considering the people we're called upon to debrief. I'll try and see to it that you've got enough time to devote to Anita and whatever meetings you'll need to finalize things with her. But you have no choice. If a meeting with Anita clashes with something I want you to do, then the meeting with Anita must suffer.'

He stopped, breathless after his lecture.

Adrian was silent for a moment, analysing the doubt that had been placed in his superior's mind by the taped interview and the reaction to it of government ministers. Was it justified? Did Anita mean more than two Russians who had a lot of space secrets? He left the questions unanswered in his mind.

'You don't have to tell me that,' he said, stiffly. 'I'm aware of my responsibilities, to you and to the department. And I recall the undertakings I gave when I joined the service.'

Binns smiled, anxious to thaw the feeling between them.

'I don't doubt you,' he said, placatory. 'I'm just sorry that personal pressure should come at a time like this.'

Adrian walked down the corridor to his own office, the realization growing of how close he had come to being removed from the debriefing. Sir Jocelyn *did* doubt him, of course, which is why he felt he had to give the warning. So the possibility still existed that he would be reassigned. He wondered if the hollowness were hunger or something else, the accusation of failure at one thing he had always been fragilely confident of doing well.

The office was empty when he entered and he looked at the clock. Miss Aimes had left forty-five minutes early. He sighed and wrote 'Miss Aimes' on the jotter, knowing he would not raise it with her the following day. Perhaps she would see it on the reminder pad and know he intended to and behave differently in the future. He knew she wouldn't do that, either. 'Soon,' he promised himself, 'I'll do something soon.'

The questions were in the safe and he glanced at them, noting the similarity to those posed to Bennovitch. He returned them, for collection the following morning on his way to Sussex and then stood, ready to leave the office.

At least Miss Aimes hadn't seen him wearing yesterday's shirt. Anita would, though, because he didn't have time to change and now the shops were closed, so he couldn't buy another one.

As he walked from the room, he looked hopefully at the window-sill, just in case. It was deserted.

'They took him out by a roundabout route,' said Kaganov. 'He went by road to Versailles and then to Brussels, by helicopter.'

'And by NATO helicopter to England,' finished Minevsky, expectantly.

The chairman nodded.

'So he's there,' mused Heirar. He sounded relieved.

'Yes.'

'How long before we seek consular access?' asked Minevsky.

'I've decided to delay it,' said Kaganov. 'I thought we'd wait a further twenty-four hours, giving a full three days.'

'Yes,' said Minevsky, 'It would probably be better.'

Heirar nodded, in silent agreement.

Chapter Four

Adrian was early, so he wandered past the flat and then down a side road, finally completing the block. He was still ahead of time. He looked inside and saw the hall porter staring at him, so he entered.

'Twenty-eight,' he said.

'The two girls,' said the man. 'Miss Sinclair and Miss Harris.'

The two girls — how ordinary and natural it sounded. She'd readopted her maiden name, he realized.

'Yes,' said Adrian.

'They expecting you?'

The porter was bristle-moustached and trying to portray the role of guardian of young innocents in London. Adrian noticed that the Military Medal ribbon on his uniform was stitched on upside down. It would be cruel to tell him.

'Yes,' he said.

'I'll check,' announced the porter, challenging Adrian to argue.

'Yes,' said Adrian, 'you'd better.'

The commissionaire replaced the house phone and said, 'Miss Harris says you're to go up.'

My wife. The contradiction echoed in Adrian's mind, like a shout. Not Miss Harris, my wife.

'Thank you,' he said.

The apartment block impressed him with its luxury. The other woman must have money. Adrian anticipated the meeting as the lift ascended, Anita guiltily shrewish,

49

the other woman mannish, probably in tweeds, hair cropped short, standing protectively over her.

No one replied when he rang the bell first and so he pressed again, his hand shaking. His finger slipped off the button. Anita answered and Adrian stood looking at her, suddenly gagged with embarrassment.

'Hello Adrian,' she said.

'Hello.'

Happiness radiated from her, like warmth, her face clean, polished almost, demure in a black sweater and contrasting oatmeal skirt. He felt a surge of emotion and wanted to kiss her. She was a slender girl, thin almost, black hair bobbed short to cup her unusually pale face. For years her doctor had treated her for anaemia before accepting her colouring as natural and only since she had been living with the other woman had she accepted the advice that Adrian had offered soon after their marriage and stopped spending half an hour a day on careful makeup.

He felt her eyes flicker over the crumpled suit, rippled with its concertina creases, and the collapsed shirt. Miss Aimes would have looked like that, the smug, knowing glance. She stood aside for him to enter the flat, a comfortable, lived-in place. There wouldn't be seats that ended halfway along his thigh, numbing his legs. He sat down and discovered he was right.

Each sat tensely, alert for the other, searching for words.

'I'm not coming back,' announced Anita abruptly.

'No,' said Adrian.

'I've thought about it and considered everything. There's only the two of us to consider. No one will be hurt,' she said.

No one? What about me? Am I no one? That mental shout of protest again.

Aloud he said, 'That's right.'

'So we've just got to accept what's happened.'

'Yes.'

'Oh, for God's sake Adrian,' she shouted, suddenly, so unexpectedly that he jumped. 'Why the hell don't you say something? I've just told you I'm never going to come back, that I'm going to live here with another woman. Isn't there any reaction? Don't you want to hit me? Don't you want to call me a whore or a queer or something? Must you accept everything that ever happens to you without protest?'

Adrian looked at her, helplessly, thoughts refusing to coalesce.

'I'm ... I'm sorry ... ' he tried, but she burst in.

'*You're* sorry. What the hell do you mean, you're sorry. I'm the one who should be apologizing, not you.'

Adrian could think of nothing to say.

'I want a divorce,' said Anita, after a pause.

'I thought you would,' said Adrian. 'I've made some inquiries already.'

'Will it be difficult?'

Adrian shook his head. 'Not really. It'll just take time. Could be as long as three years, maybe more, because we haven't been living apart for very long.'

'What have I got to do?'

'Nothing,' he said. 'I'll make all the arrangements. Just get a solicitor and let me know who he is, so our solicitors can start communicating.'

'Will there have to be grounds, evidence ... details about what's happened?'

'No, I don't think so, not in open court. Our solicitors will have to know, of course.'

'If it's necessary to provide grounds, would you do it?' she asked, suddenly, her attitude meek and pleading now.

'What?' he frowned, unsure of the question.

'If there have to be grounds, like adultery or something, couldn't you pay a prostitute or something like that?'

He looked at her, shocked, not because of her presump-

51

tion, but her assumption that he would go with a whore.

'Well, will you?'

'I've told you, it's not necessary, the only reason for divorce now is the irretrievable breakdown of a marriage. And ours certainly qualifies.'

'Sure?'

'Yes.'

'But if you're wrong, you'll provide the grounds?'

He'd never completely realized the depth of her selfishness before.

'Yes,' he said wearily. 'Yes, I'll provide the grounds.'

She nodded, satisfied. Bottles were in a trolley shaped like a miniature horsecart, near the window. She saw him looking at them.

'Oh, would you like a drink, or something?'

'No, no thank you.'

'Some food? When did you last eat?'

She looked at his clothes, again recognizing the neglect. 'No, really. I couldn't eat a thing,' he lied. 'I had a meal before I came here.'

The door lock grated and they stopped, both looking expectantly at the entrance. Adrian saw a tall, willowy girl enter, long blonde hair looped to her shoulders. She was small-busted but surprisingly attractive. She wore a brown cashmere sweater under a Chanel suit and had hardly any makeup on. Adrian thought she was quite lovely.

'Oh,' she said, smiling, her teeth perfect. 'Hello.'

Adrian was confused, mentally prepared for tweeds and mannishness, suddenly confronted by such obvious femininity. Did that mean that Anita was ... ?

'Anne,' said Anita, easily, 'this is Adrian.'

She stayed smiling and reached out. Hesitatingly he took her hand. The shake was soft and womanlike.

'She won't bite you, Adrian,' said Anita. 'We don't all wear trousers and smoke pipes, you know.'

'Don't, Anita,' rebuked Anne Sinclair.

'Hello,' said Adrian, remaining standing. He was aware of the feeling between the two women. He felt like a Peeping Tom.

'Oh, do sit down,' she said. 'Has Anita offered you a drink? Some brandy? Or some wine perhaps? We've got some in the fridge.'

At Eton Adrian had twice a year gone to tea in his housemaster's study and been served slightly burned scones and weak tea by the man's wife.

She had recognized his shyness and favoured him just slightly above the other boys, giving him, just once every six months, thirty minutes of favoured attention, listening to him intently, as if what *he* said mattered, drawing opinions from him and then deferring to them and Adrian had thought she was the most wonderful woman in the world. He found himself comparing her to the blonde woman before him.

'Yes ... no,' said Adrian, blushing under the attention. 'She's offered me a drink, but I refused ... '

'Are you sure?'

'Adrian doesn't want to put us to any inconvenience, not even one duty glass,' said Anita, the jeer quite clear.

'Do stop it, Anita,' said Anne. She turned to Adrian. 'Did you have any difficulty finding the flat?' she said, pleasantly. 'We gave a housewarming the other night and some people took hours to get here.'

Just like the housemaster's tea party. A cosy room, pleasant, easily handled small talk, like a friendly game of table tennis where you lob the ball over the net towards the other person's bat.

'No, not really. I thought it was quite easy,' said Adrian. They'd probably discuss the weather and that year's holiday, he thought. He controlled a snigger at the stupidity of it, the social conversation with his wife's lover. Unasked, Anita poured a brandy and took it to the other girl, who accepted it without thanks, acknowledging a well established ritual. For a few seconds they looked at one another and Adrian felt an interloper again.

'We're going to have some supper in a while,' said Anne, turning back to him. 'Why don't you stay?'

'Thank you, that's very kind ... ' began Adrian, but his wife cut in. 'But he can't,' said Anita. 'He's already eaten and couldn't manage another thing.'

'Yes,' agreed Adrian, reminded. 'I've already eaten. And I have a couple of things to do tonight.'

His stomach yawned at the thought of food.

Anita is enjoying my discomfort, thought Adrian, suddenly. The bitch is gloating, happy at her odd security, enjoying my crumpled suit and filthy shirt and knowing I haven't eaten. She probably even guesses there weren't any eggs for breakfast.

'You're staring at me,' grinned Anne and if he had been unaware of the circumstances, Adrian would have said she was flirting with him.

'Oh, I'm sorry,' he said, flushing and regretting it. Anita suddenly became aware of the exchange and Adrian saw her go white. He wondered if Anne were playing some odd sort of love game.

Anita began to talk, trying to reduce her husband before the other woman.

'Adrian at his best,' she said, 'apologizing.' Anne said nothing, merely holding up an empty glass which Anita hurriedly took from her and refilled. Adrian realized that despite her apparent femininity, Anne was the dominant character. Oddly, he felt regret.

'I think I'd better get going,' he said.

'Oh, really,' said Anne. 'Surely you can stay on a little longer? Why not change your mind and have a meal?'

'He has to go,' said Anita, the jealousy obvious.

To her Adrian said, 'You'll let me have the address of a solicitor?'

It occurred to him that it would have been easier for them to arrange the whole thing by letter. It had been Anita who had insisted on the meeting and he suddenly realized she had purposely schemed his humiliation with Anne, creating the comparison between two rivals.

'Yes,' said Anita. 'I'll give you a solicitor's name.'

'You have my new number, in case you want to call me,' said Adrian, still feeling sympathy.

His wife nodded.

'Goodbye,' he said, to Anne. She smiled and walked with him to the door.

'Maybe I'll see you again.'

'Maybe,' he said, automatically.

Downstairs the lift gave its tiny bump and Adrian emerged into the lobby. The porter grinned. 'Not staying long,' he said, as if he knew.

Adrian started to ignore him, and then stopped. 'That the Military Medal?' he asked. The porter smiled, preparing himself for the rehearsed speech. Adrian cut him off. 'It's on upside down,' he said. It wasn't a great victory, but Adrian walked out into the night nursing a small feeling of contentment.

'I've had an idea,' said Minevsky. Actually it had occurred to him several days before, but he had waited, assessing the moment of maximum impact.

'What?' asked Kaganov.

'Why don't we expel a British diplomat? We can create a situation around one of the embassy staff. London is sure to retaliate and expel one of our men. It will keep everything boiling.'

'Good idea,' conceded Heirar, reluctantly. 'Who'll it be?'

Minevsky shrugged. 'Doesn't really matter. I suppose the military attaché is the most obvious choice.'

'All right,' said Kaganov. 'Let's use the military attaché.'

'What's his name?' asked Minevsky, not really wanting to know, but anxious to extend the recording. The other two men stared at him, curiously. 'Haven't the slightest idea,' said Kaganov. 'It doesn't matter, does it?'

'No,' agreed Minevsky. 'Of course not.'

Chapter Five

It was planned for surprise effect, the second interview coming as a complete contrast to the first, concentrating completely upon technicalities and conducted in a formal, rigid pattern, calculated to shatter any rehearsed reaction.

A defector was never accepted as genuine until at least six debriefing sessions.

Pavel had expected to continue the bickering of the previous day, but Adrian curtailed him brusquely. He spoke almost as if they had never met, sitting with the clipboard of questions before him, isolating himself completely from any dissension, a cipher almost.

'I have a list of questions,' he began. 'I'm sorry, but I am not a technical man, so I will have to refer to these notes. I won't, of course, be annotating your answers ... '

' ... Because of the recorders ... ' He was still laughing. Adrian ignored the invitation.

'How many Soyuz missions have there been?'

'But you must know that. They have all been made public. Surely you don't think we've put some up without announcement? I thought your monitoring stations were better than that.'

'How many Soyuz missions have there been?' repeated Adrian, doggedly.

'Fifteen.'

'Tell me about your suitings.'

'Very similar to the American Apollo EMP-A-7lbs for intravehicular operations. The suit design for extra-vehicular activity is almost identical to the EV-A-7lbs of the American Apollo 15 mission, but with a back-pack lighter by about two pounds.'

It wasn't on the form before him, but Adrian knew the questions would be asked, so he said, 'You seem well informed of the Apollo equipment. How?' Pavel lounged in one of the leather armchairs, completely at ease.

'America is such an open society,' he mocked. 'Did you know that Apollo 15 had a 157-page press kit, as well as technical releases to trade press and experts?'

'No,' said Adrian.

'Any enterprising diplomat in Washington can work full time ferrying information back which the Americans seem only too anxious for everyone to know.'

Adrian pictured the reaction that remark would cause among the C.I.A. when they got a recording. 'What space suit changes were made following the Soyuz disaster?'

Pavel laughed. 'We announced that, too. Our cosmonauts no longer re-enter the atmosphere after a mission without suits, in case of minuscule oxygen leaks.'

Adrian flicked a page and Pavel said, 'Why this change of attitude?'

Adrian didn't answer.

'Complaints about the way yesterday's interview went?' he persevered with uncanny accuracy.

'I'd like to talk about the equipment on moon probes,' said Adrian.

'Wasn't anybody distressed at our obvious antipathy?'

Pavel was over-stressing the mockery. Did that show over-concern?

'Are any more moon probes planned?'

Pavel shrugged, apparently accepting the mechanical responses of his interrogator.

'Three,' he answered. 'None will be manned. We plan a much bigger version of the American mooncar and much more sophisticated than our first one. It will be fitted with more automatic rock collecting and measuring devices.'

'How much bigger?'

'The American L.V.R. was small, only ten feet two inches long, with a 7.5-foot wheelbase powered over individual wheels with a quarter-horsepower electric motor. Ours will be at least twenty feet over a comparable wheelbase and have a midwheel section, giving total wheeling of twelve feet. It will have a payload capability of 2,670 pounds. The American only had 1,080 pounds, including astronauts.'

'Electrically powered?'

Pavel shook his head. 'Solar systemed, with an earth-operated electrical back-up system.'

'How are you going to boost a thing that size into orbit?'

Pavel laughed again. 'Typical earthbound question,' he jeered. 'Who says you've got to construct it on the ground?'

'Meaning?'

'Meaning the rover vehicle, which will have a cabin rather like a caravan in which a man could operate without any protection whatsoever, will leave earth on a rocket much smaller than that of the Americans. It'll be assembled in space in an orbiting laboratory.'

Adrian paused. Everything Bennovitch had said was confirmed. But there was nothing new. 'What else will be the function of the lunar caravan?'

'Solar wind composition experiments, to determine the isoptric makeup of inert gases in the wind, and it will also include a laser retro-reflector to act as a passive target for earth-based lasers for calculation over a long period.'

'The Americans have organized similar experiments during the Apollo series. Isn't it wasteful duplicating exchange-material tests?'

'It's only surface duplication,' said Pavel. 'The adaptation of the results could differ.'

59

'What does that mean?' asked Adrian, departing from the form again.

'The Americans are still a long way from establishing a space platform. Don't always look to the end of the experiment for its ultimate worth. The success of a moon rover — whether it functions, the incidence of errors — will indicate whether or not we can successfully create something in space.'

A hint? Adrian continued the line that Pavel had opened. 'Is there a Russian plan to establish a space platform for military purposes?'

Pavel laughed, that jeering sound again, and Adrian felt he had been drawn too far, tricked into asking a stupid question.

'Why do you have to begin every question with the supposition that Russia is the villain, pursuing the virginity of the rest of the world?'

'That's an exaggeration. I wouldn't have expected that from a scientific mind,' countered Adrian. 'It's an obvious question, when we talk of space platforms capable of building lunar caravans.'

'What about forecasting?' asked Pavel, carelessly.

'Unnecessary,' countered Adrian again, quickly. 'All necessary weather information can be obtained from unmanned satellites.'

'True,' conceded Pavel. 'What about astrological research?'

'Unnecessary again,' said Adrian. 'You can conduct those probes as well from unmanned stations.'

'I've got you away from the listed questions,' said Pavel and laughed, an excited sound, like a trainer who had encouraged a seal to balance a ball.

Adrian flushed, bending back to the clipboard. 'Let's talk about space photography,' he said.

'As you wish,' said Pavel, condescendingly. Adrian jerked up. The other man had replied in Russian.

'As *you* wish,' responded Adrian, lapsing easily into the same language. He supposed Pavel had done it to discomfit him, but he was utterly sure of his language control.

'Are you interested in Gegenschein?' Adrian recited.

'Do you know what Gegenschein is?' mocked Pavel.

'The faint light source covering a 20-degree field of view along the earth-sun line on the opposite side of the earth from the sun,' replied Adrian, immediately. He looked up. 'The questions are listed to prompt me,' he said. 'I try *awfully* hard to escape portraying myself as a complete cretin.'

Adrian was glad they had lapsed into Russian. Irony sounded so much more vitriolic. Pavel nodded, accepting the rebuke.

'The next probe will have electrically controlled cameras, working with a 55-mm. lens at $F/1.2$ on high-speed black and white. It's essentially dim-light photography. We are inclined to accept the theory that the origin of Gegenschein is particles of matter trapped at the Moulton Point, reflecting sunlight. You know what the Moulton Point is?'

He wasn't relaxing for a moment, thought Adrian. 'Yes,' he replied. 'The theoretical point 940,000 statute miles from earth along the anti-solar axis where the sum of all gravitational forces is zero.'

'Bet you were the top boy in the class,' mocked Pavel.

'Alpha-plus every time,' replied Adrian.

'Or perhaps you've absorbed a lot. Alexandre must have been very forthcoming.'

Adrian didn't reply, but marked the response on his clipsheet for later examination when the tape was transcribed. He felt there had been a little too much eagerness in Pavel's reaction, too much artifice in trying to annoy with sarcasm, then following up with a question which could have brought out any angry, unconsidered reply. Pavel went on. 'Can I see Alexandre?'

'Of course.'

'When?'

'In a while.'

'After you've drawn all the material possible from me?'

Adrian smiled. The other man was remarkably well informed about debriefing procedure. 'Yes,' he smiled.

'How long will that take?'

'Depends on how long our debriefing sessions last.' The Russian-speaking guards entered with coffee, and for a few moments they stopped talking. Adrian waited, putting a theory to the test. It was Pavel who broke the silence.

'We could talk and take our coffee at the same time.'

Adrian nodded, happy at the outcome. For the next three hours they talked, ranging over future Russian moon exploration from passive seismic experiments, suprathermal ion detection and cold cathode gauge probes to planned geology investigations and then covering, point by point, the equipment that would be provided in the space platforms and mooncraft.

Adrian stopped at one-thirty. No cooked meal for forty-eight hours he thought, as he looked at his watch.

'We made progress today,' said Pavel.

'Yes.'

'Will I see you tomorrow?'

'Yes, but I have to stop on the way here, so I won't arrive until eleven-thirty.'

'Oh, so he's quite near here.'

Adrian had his back to the Russian, storing clipboard and questions into the briefcase with the numbered combination lock, so the surprise was concealed.

'Who?' he parried.

'Alexandre, of course,' said Pavel, irritably. 'Who else would you be seeing? Will you tell him about me?'

'I don't know.'

'No, I suppose there's not a lot of point. You've got all

62

you want from him, so there's nothing to be gained in using my defection as a bargaining point or shock revelation.'

'I can't recall telling you that we've got everything from Bennovitch.'

'Haven't you then?'

A fraction too quick, judged Adrian. He didn't reply to the Russian's question. Perhaps detecting his own eagerness, Pavel did not repeat it.

Again Adrian drove leisurely back to London. It would not be possible for them to hear the full tape, but he would give them sufficient time to realize progress was being made.

He thought about Anita, wedged in that cramped City office, typing out shipboard invoices and cargo manifests. She had said Anne Sinclair worked in the same building. But not a typist, judged Adrian, easing the car through Vauxhall. No, Anne Sinclair didn't fit the role. She'd be a personal secretary, super-efficient, shouldering a lot of responsibility, friendly yet just a little bit too aloof from any office Romeo who tried to create any relationship. He wondered if anyone there knew of the association between the two women, guessed from intercepting a glance or seeing a half hidden gesture. Probably not. Anne Sinclair wouldn't let that happen because it would reveal a failing and Adrian didn't think she was a girl who admitted to any failings.

Miss Aimes was in the office when he entered and carefully locked away the briefcase.

'He hasn't come back,' she reported.

Adrian was momentarily confused.

'Who?'

'The pigeon.'

'Oh.'

He felt her looking at his creased suit. At least the shirt was fresh.

63

'Your wife away?'

'What?'

'I asked if your wife was away.'

Why should he reply? The relationship between them had always been strictly businesslike, so there was no encouragement to impertinence, sarcasm veiled in what appeared a casual inquiry. He should put her in her place, immediately.

'Yes,' he lied instead. 'As a matter of fact she is. Her mother ... her mother is ill. She's gone to the country to look after her.'

'Oh.' The woman took another look at the suit.

'Any messages?'

'Sir Jocelyn wants to see you at three-thirty,' said the secretary. 'I've typed yesterday's debriefing, and the resulting questions have come across from the Technical Section.'

'Thank you.'

'There was a note on your reminder pad.'

'What?'

'On your reminder pad, you'd written my name. Was there something you wanted to talk to me about?'

Adrian recalled her early departure from the office the previous evening and the resolution to make a protest to re-establish his position with the woman. He turned. Inevitably she was patting those rigid iron grey furrows. He wondered if he would ever satisfy his curiosity about that hairpiece.

'No,' he said. 'It was nothing.'

'Sure?' she asked.

'Yes, quite sure.'

The cleared line from Binns buzzed and Adrian picked up the grey telephone.

'How did it go?' asked the Permanent Secretary.

'Better,' said Adrian. 'Haven't you heard all the tape?'

'Up to the moment he lapsed into Russian.'

Adrian had forgotten the language change. It would mean translation and cause several hours' delay.

'He was much more forthcoming,' he said.

'Well, that's progress.'

'I'm not sure,' said Adrian.

'What?'

'I'll explain it when we meet.'

'That's the point of this call,' said Binns. 'This thing is creating the most incredible international outcry from practically everyone. We've even had some of our men expelled from Moscow now, alleging that we are actually enticing their scientists across. It's far far worse than when Oleg Lyalin defected and we expelled the majority of their Trade Mission. America has been asked to pressure us privately to return both Bennovitch and Pavel, in return for future closer space co-operation. The Russians have even offered to let some people from Houston visit Baikonur ... '

'I don't believe it would ever come off,' interrupted Adrian.

'Neither do I,' picked up Binns. 'But it's an impressive offer and the Americans are nibbling hard at the bait.'

'What else?'

'Every newspaper in the world is advancing every sort of speculation you can imagine on the importance of these two. The Prime Minister wants to see us this afternoon.'

Adrian looked down at his creased suit. He wouldn't have time to have it pressed.

'The Prime Minister?' he queried.

'Yes,' said Binns. 'He's taken over personal control.'

'Oh,' said Adrian. 'What time does he want to see us?'

'Four,' said Binns. 'So you'd better come across here at three to brief me fully before the meeting.'

Adrian replaced the receiver and saw Miss Aimes smiling across the desk at him.

'Going all afternoon?' she asked.

He nodded, aware she was planning another early night. Perhaps tomorrow. Perhaps then he'd talk to her.

'Let's review what we've done so far,' said Kaganov, an unnecessary list of reminders before him. 'Because Pavel defected in Paris, we've protested to France and threatened the cancellation of the trade agreement negotiated by Pompidou. We've made every official protest to Britain, brought pressure through Washington with the Baikonur promise, recalled our ambassador to London for consultations and expelled the British military attaché and two first secretaries.'

'It was brilliant to hint the attaché was in some way involved with enticing both men over,' admitted Minevsky. The move had earned a lot of praise, but people were forgetting it was his idea.

'Is there anything else that needs doing to keep it bubbling?' said Heirar. 'We can't allow the tension to relax for a moment. Who's debriefing Pavel? Do we know?'

'Of course,' said Kaganov. 'It's the man the British always use. His name is Adrian Dodds. According to our embassy, he's quite brilliant.'

'Shouldn't we do something there?' continued Heirar. 'Shouldn't we move against him?'

'Good God, no,' said Minevsky, anticipating by a few seconds the reaction that would come from the chairman.

'What the hell are you suggesting?' took up Kaganov.

Heirar pressed on. 'Surely we could stage-manage an attempted assassination?'

'You must be mad,' said Minevsky. 'They'd immediately take Dodds away from the debriefing. It could take the embassy weeks to discover who his replacement would be. And anyway, we only know his name. We don't know his identity or *where* he is.'

66

Chapter Six

Adrian and Sir Jocelyn walked from their office, threading their way through the labyrinth of passages at the rear of the Foreign Office. They ignored the front entrance of Downing Street, going down the steps to loop back through Horseguards Parade to enter, from habit, through the rear entrance.

In St James's Park, sun worshippers were prostrate on the grass and Adrian studied them enviously. No worries, he thought. No broken marriages, no be-wigged secretaries, no laundry problems. And they'd have eaten as well.

Both knew the inside of the Prime Minister's official house from previous visits and confidently followed the male secretary through the corridors and into the small office off the larger Cabinet Room.

Although they were ten minutes early, the Prime Minister and the Foreign Secretary were waiting.

'Here you are, here you are,' said the Premier, Arnold Ebbetts, impatiently, as if they were at least an hour late for the appointment.

He was a fat, fleshy man, who affected a pipe he rarely lit and the sort of tweed suits that cost thirty pounds from multiple tailors and could be recognized as such. He culti-vated a reputation for bluntness, which he practised when it would cause no harm, and always invited the press to his summer cottage in Yorkshire for duty pictures of him with flat cap and briar stick, a man of the people who'd made good but hadn't forgotten his humble origins of grammar school and Barnsley Technical College. He had a mind like a computer, an ambition to be remembered as one of Britain's ablest premiers and rarely in public speeches did he forget to drop his aitches.

Arnold Ebbetts was a politician's politician. The man he most admired was Arnold Ebbetts.

'Here you are,' echoed the Foreign Minister. Predictably, Adrian felt sorry for him. Sir William Fornham was a cartoonist's dream, a caricature of a British aristocrat, so that people judged him — quite wrongly — from a commentator's drawing rather than his performance. He was a tall, bony man, who had forsaken his hereditary title to serve his country, which he did well but for which he got little recognition. He suffered the disadvantage of believing through tradition, breeding and education that all men were gentlemen who told the truth and was constantly offended to discover otherwise. Apart from that his only other failing was that he often appeared to be thinking of something else, which he wasn't, and so to prove his attention he had developed the habit of repeating the final five or six words of the person who spoke before him.

He was Foreign Secretary because the government needed a man of wealth to capture the intellectual right wing of the party. Sir William was aware of it, but he knew his worth and was prepared to be used by an ambitious prime minister because it had been the role of his family for three centuries to serve their country. History, hoped Sir William, would correctly assess his contribution to be as great as that of any of his ancestors.

Ebbetts had decided upon bluntness.

'What the hell's going on?' he demanded, looking at Adrian. 'Don't like the way this debriefing is going, don't like it at all.'

Sir William reserved judgment by failing to pick up the end of the sentence.

'What don't you like?'

Adrian felt the glance of Sir Jocelyn at the lack of respect and mentally shrugged it aside. He *was* right about Pavel. He knew he was. And he knew that time would prove him correct. He hoped he could maintain his attitude throughout the meeting.

'You're handling the man wrong, all wrong,' said Ebbetts. 'He's hostile. And we haven't got time to muck about. Speed is the element here.'

' ... element here,' intoned Sir William.

'But why?' queried Adrian. 'I'm sure Sir Jocelyn has made it clear that speed is just the thing to avoid in a debriefing. Answers have got to be checked, then cross-checked, then analysed ... '

'Rubbish.' The Premier cut him off with a wave of his hand. 'Is Bennovitch genuine?'

'Yes,' replied Adrian, 'I believe he is.'

'Is Pavel genuine?'

'Depends what you mean by genuine,' countered Adrian.

'Don't play with me, Dodds,' said Ebbetts, irritably. 'Say what you mean.'

'I believe the man who defected to our embassy in Paris and whom I have spent two days debriefing in Sussex is Viktor Pavel, who, with Alexandre Bennovitch, forms Russia's most important space team,' replied Adrian, formally. He was irritated by the posturing of the other man and determined not to be pressured.

'What then?' asked the Premier and Sir William came in with 'What then?'

'I am suspicious of the man ... ' began Adrian, but the Premier cut him off. 'I know, I know. I've heard from Binns all about your impressions that don't have an ounce of evidence to back them up.'

Adrian sighed, feeling that the Premier had made up his mind on a course of action before the meeting began.

He tried again. 'In any defector, the impressions, the

feelings, if you like, that you are dismissing so quickly are important. Often men who are anxious to get asylum give the impression that their importance is far greater than it is … '

'For God's sake, man, Viktor Pavel is probably the cleverest space scientist Russia has ever produced … the cleverest man there's been for years. He'd make Einstein look like a fifth-former. Bennovitch is important, but even he doesn't compare. You've said that yourself. We can't begin to challenge Pavel's knowledge because we haven't got anyone in this country, or in the West for that matter, on the same level. What the hell's all this talk about "impressions of importance"?'

Adrian experienced a wave of nervousness and tried to subdue it. This meeting could decide his future with the department.

'I'm sorry,' he said. 'I'm expressing myself badly, but I meant to go on, beyond that. I'm not questioning Pavel's brilliance. I'm not questioning, either, the incredible value he could have for Western space advances. I'm unsure of the motives of the man in coming across.'

'What other motives can a man have when he runs to the embassy of a foreign country and begs asylum?'

'I don't believe Pavel wants to defect,' Adrian blurted out, accepting the stupidity of the words as he uttered them, desperation moving his tongue ahead of his thoughts.

'Wants to defect?' queried the Prime Minister and when Sir William echoed 'Wants to defect?' the incredulity indicated greater feeling than he usually expressed.

'What Dodds means, I think,' said Sir Jocelyn, trying to come to his assistant's aid, 'is that some uncertainty has arisen in Pavel since he crossed over. You've read the transcripts. The uncertainty is obviously there.' The nerve irritated under his eye.

'Any uncertainty that has arisen in Pavel is the direct

result of the way he's been treated, in my opinion,' snapped Ebbetts.

' ... way he's been treated ... ' came from Sir William.

Adrian laid his hands flat on the table, looking down for concentration. The meeting was falling away from him. He was appearing a rambling fool.

'Please,' he said, the desperation edging in again. 'Please let me speak, for a moment, without interruption, so that I can try and communicate completely what I feel.'

He paused. The other men stayed silent. Even in complete silence, Ebbetts seemed to be challenging him.

'Certainly it's possible,' he began, 'for a defector — for Pavel — to experience a change of heart. In fact, it is ridiculous for him to expect and for us to expect that some doubt, some homesickness or guilt, won't arise. Bennovitch said, as you'll have heard from his recordings, that he felt guilty and had some regrets. But for him it was easy, because he had no family upon whom he knew retribution would be carried out. Pavel protected his sister. Any defector with a family knows that they will be made pariahs in the Soviet Union. Pavel is an intelligent man, someone who deeply loves his family. According to Bennovitch, Pavel's only interest, apart from his work, was his wife and two children. Imagine what's going to happen to that woman now — first her brother, then her husband, together the two most important men in the Russian space programme. It will be a miracle if she doesn't face trial ... '

'I've tried to be patient,' burst in Ebbetts, 'but I can't see the point you're trying to make. Of course we all know what is likely to happen to Pavel's wife ... that it will probably be far worse than what happens to relatives of most defectors ... '

'And that's exactly the point,' said Adrian, with the vehemence of a man who has scored an advantage in a debate. 'Pavel *knows* what will happen to her. And he

71

knew it before he even considered coming across. Is that the action of a man deeply devoted to his wife? Would such a man abandon a woman he loves to a life sentence in a labour camp at Potma?'

'But he *has*,' pointed out Ebbetts. 'I accept the point you're making and I agree that if this had been a hypothetical discussion on the likelihood of Pavel following Bennovitch, then I would have agreed completely with you and dismissed as ludicrous the merest suggestion that Pavel would defect. But he *has* defected. You're arguing philosophy. I'm arguing facts.'

'Wait,' pleaded Adrian. 'Please wait. Knowing, upon your acceptance of my point, that his wife would be punished, Pavel goes ahead and defects. And then, belatedly, becomes covered with remorse. You've seen the reports of the men guarding him, you've read the transcripts of the conversations he has had with them ... '

Ebbetts staged a theatrical sigh.

Adrian hesitated, then forced himself on. 'I've rarely known a more painstaking man. He flies into a rage if a cleaner so much as moves a hair-brush an inch from where he's decided it should rest. Twice he's carried out an entire inventory against the list he's prepared and always has with him of what he's been allowed to keep in his room ... '

Another sigh. 'Get on with it, man,' implored Ebbetts.

'It's an analytical mind,' said Adrian. 'He thinks, considers, makes notes and refers to them ... he's painfully old womanish, if you like. But the point is he calculates everything *before* he moves, not afterwards. For Pavel to become concerned about what effect his defection will have upon his wife and family *after* he's come across is so out of character and unreal as to be suspicious.'

'Psychological poppycock,' dismissed Ebbetts.

'And there's more,' went on Adrian. 'I believe Sir Jocelyn has told you about the man's attitude ... '

72

'Resulting from your own. A man reacts in attitude to the way he's treated,' interrupted the Premier, quoting elementary Dale Carnegie.

Adrian was breathing heavily, losing ground. He could feel perspiration rivering beneath his shirt.

'No, that's not it,' he said. 'Listen to the first tape again, please. Pavel's attitude was formed from our first word. Over-confident and protective ... '

'Protective.' Ebbetts seized the word, rushing in like a ferret. 'That's just it. Wouldn't you be protective, wouldn't you be afraid but try not to show it if you'd defected to Moscow? I'm amazed, I really am. I'd had the highest regard for your ability, Dodds, until now. You've had courses in psychology and according to what Binns tells me, one of the commonest indications of fear or inferiority is a show of shallow self-confidence.'

'But Pavel's self-confidence isn't shallow. I've debriefed defectors before who've shown the symptoms you talk about. I can recognize that sort of confidence within minutes. And it usually evaporates within the first hour of the initial meeting. Pavel *is* confident.'

'And why the hell shouldn't he be?' asked Ebbetts. 'He's a genius. And he knows it. He can look upon this initial debriefing as a formality, the necessary form-filling, like taking out a television licence at a post office ... '

Ebbetts paused and smiled. 'No disrespect to your role, of course, but that's what it is. He knows our technical men are dying to get their hands on him and he'll know the Americans feel the same way. Usually your defectors are frightened, unsure of their worth. That's exactly the reason Pavel isn't frightened. He's led a pampered life in Russia for nearly twenty years which tells him just how valuable he is. Good God man, you've heard of prima donnas, haven't you? That's what Pavel is, a conceited prima donna.'

Yes, thought Adrian, I've heard of prima donnas. He

73

shook his head in disagreement with Ebbetts's opinion, but said nothing. Ebbetts knew he had destroyed the other man's argument and carried on, the bully emerging at the recognition of a weaker character.

'All right,' he said. 'Let's examine your points.'

He stood up and splayed his fingers, like a schoolmaster addressing a backward class.

'Point one — Pavel adores his family and would never leave them behind for harassment by the Russians. Answer — he has. I don't care if it's out of character. I don't care if Pavel makes notes of everything, even about going to the lavatory before he does it. The fact which cannot be ignored is that Pavel deserted his family. Point two — he's not nervous, but just the opposite, insufferably self-confident. Answer — he's got every right to be.'

A heavy silence settled in the room. Adrian sat, realizing his objections had been reduced to nonsense. He'd lost. Again.

Ebbetts continued in the role of politician, winning back a man he'd just defeated.

'Let's face it, Dodds,' he began, his voice placatory now. 'People don't run on train lines, starting out from one spot in their character and then continuing in a straight, predictable line. That's what human nature is, people behaving in an unexpected way. You're surprised that Pavel has come across and can't accept it. I'm surprised he's come across and I can accept it. And the facts as we know them at the moment indicate that my assessment is right, don't they?'

Adrian refused to give up without a struggle. 'On the facts as we know them at the moment,' he said.

Ebbetts frowned, angrily. He had been walking up and down the small office, an unsettling trick he had perfected, so that people had to move their heads back and forth, like a Wimbledon tennis audience. He stopped, leaning across the table towards Adrian, the determination to crush obvious.

'All right,' he said, his voice over-controlled. 'Let's argue your objections to their ultimate, illogical conclusion. If you're convinced that Pavel is here for some underlying reason, then you must have decided what that reason is. Are you suggesting that Pavel is here in the role of an assassin, to liquidate a former partner?'

'No, I ... '

'What then?'

Ebbetts was being quite merciless, enjoying it even. Adrian wondered how much training it needed to develop the hardness, the disregard of everything except the need to win every discussion and point, no matter how trivial.

'What then?' echoed Sir William and Adrian looked at him in surprise. He'd almost forgotten his presence.

Adrian shrugged. 'I don't know,' he said.

Ebbetts used that sigh again, the sneer more eloquent than any words.

'Right,' he said. 'Now we've dispensed with any doubt about Pavel, let's start thinking objectively.'

He had resumed his pacing back and forth, but now he stopped, sitting down immediately opposite the debriefing team.

'I know all about your usual procedures for debriefing, but this is an unusual case, a very unusual case, so we're going to have to depart from routine.'

' ... depart from routine,' came from the Premier's right.

'We're under pressure, intense pressure,' continued Ebbetts. 'To hear the Russians talk, you'd think they're going back to Berlin and the Cold War. I thought the Lyalin case was bad enough, but it was child's play compared to this. Trouble is, the Americans seem to be backing the Soviets. Washington is very attracted by the Baikonur

75

bait. If we don't move quickly, there'll be a major shift in friendships and we don't want that.'

'What do you want?' asked Binns. Adrian realized how quiet the Permanent Secretary had been throughout the meeting. By his refusal to help, Sir Jocelyn was obviously expressing his agreement with the Prime Minister over the Pavel assessment.

'I want Pavel debriefed quickly, more quickly than you've ever processed anyone before. I want the two men, Pavel and Bennovitch, thrown together. They're friends. It'll be a great psychological move, make them feel more relaxed, more ready to help ... '

He looked directly at Adrian.

'I am not taking you off this debriefing,' he said. 'Normally, I would. I repeat the point I made earlier. I think you've conducted it extremely badly. But speed is the key factor here and I don't want to waste time on introducing another interrogator. That would lose two, maybe three days. But listen to what I say — I don't want to waste time. You're to eradicate completely from your mind and your attitudes and your questions any hint of doubt about Pavel or his intentions in defecting. Is that clear?'

'Yes,' replied Adrian, meekly.

'I want to be able to promise Washington that their men can get to both Pavel and Bennovitch within a fortnight. The Americans want to go to Baikonur, but they want Pavel and Bennovitch even more. If I can give them a definite date, then we'll keep the Americans on our side.'

He smiled, a conjuror about to produce his best trick.

'And if Pavel and Bennovitch go to America, then the bad feeling goes with them. So we'll have all the space knowledge that the two men possess, America will be indebted to us for years and Russia will switch its anger and resume normal relations with us in about six months.'

Despite his antipathy for Ebbetts, Adrian had to admire the reasoning. He sat, envying the man and his force-fulness. Anita would have admired it too. If he'd had the character of Ebbetts, then Anita would still be with him now, admiring him even, content to be dominated.

Adrian jumped, realizing Ebbetts was addressing him. 'I said, any questions?' repeated the Prime Minister, irritably.

'No,' said Adrian. 'No questions.'

He paused, and it was obvious that he intended continuing, so they remained looking at him. 'But I'd like to make a point, just one. I accept, from this afternoon's meeting, how the stupidity of my doubts has been shown up ... '

The Prime Minister smiled and made a deprecating gesture with his hands as if, unthinkably, even he had made mistakes on rare occasions.

' ... I accept completely the instructions I have been given. Pavel and Bennovitch will be thrown together, the debriefing will be speeded up and I shall do every-thing within my power to ensure we extract the maximum information before they are offered the opportunity of going to America, with the attraction of a space pro-gramme to work upon ... '

'I admire your attitude,' said Ebbetts, smiling.

'But let me say this,' went on Adrian, his voice rising above the monotone in which he had been speaking. 'I still believe I am right. Although it will not be evident from my subsequent examination of either man, my suspicion remains. I believe that something will happen, something which none of us can guess at this moment. I believe what I have been told to do is wrong. I should be allowed more time.'

He stopped, his stomach bubbling. For the first time in his life, Adrian Dodds had taken a position opposing that of the majority. He had expressed an opinion which isolated him from everyone, and put him in the spotlight. He had considered the outburst, at first dismissing the idea as ludicrous, but then he had realized that although he was being kept on the debriefing, for the sake of expediency, Sir Jocelyn would be told within hours to seek and train a new assistant.

Adrian had accepted his dismissal from the department even before he received it, and he realized that there was nothing he could lose by honesty. He had therefore decided, for the first time in his life, to express himself instead of stifling what he was really thinking, even if it clashed with the view of everyone else.

He had expected to feel euphoria, the self-satisfaction of knowing he was right against all opposition. Instead he felt sick and he wanted to use a toilet. He sat there with the three men staring at him as if he had mouthed an obscenity in a monastery, and wished more fervently than he ever had wanted anything before that he had kept his mouth shut.

'I think,' said Ebbetts, stiffly, 'that this meeting is over.'

Pompously, he walked from the room, trailed by the Foreign Secretary.

As they walked back to their office, Adrian said, 'I'm sorry. I know I've let you down. And the department too.'

Binns did not reply. His face twitched.

'This will be my last debriefing, won't it?'

'I expect so,' said Binns, controlling the stutter with difficulty. He isn't at ease with me any more, thought Adrian. I've lost his friendship.

'I really am sorry,' he repeated.

'It can't be helped. It's done now.'

'I regret letting you down, personally.'

Binns shrugged. 'What will you do?'

'I don't know,' said Adrian. 'There's nothing else I can do.'

They entered the maze behind the Foreign Office,

leaving the sunbathers in St James's Park still unworried.

'I believe I am right,' said Adrian.

'Obviously,' said Binns. 'But was one opinion worth destroying a career?'

'No,' agreed Adrian, back into character again. 'No, it wasn't.'

Yes, he thought, yes it was. The sickness had disappeared, but he still wanted a lavatory. Badly.

Chapter Seven

Binns looked grey and his eyes were red with strain. Adrian realized as he walked into the other man's office the morning after their meeting with the Prime Minister that the Permanent Secretary had not slept.

'I've read everything,' began Binns, tapping the grey folders on the desk before him. 'The histories, Bennovitch's complete debriefing and your assessment, the debriefing of Pavel, all the protests and assessments by our experts and all the reports from the security officers guarding both men.'

The speech impediment was still there. So the gap remained between them. Adrian waited for Binns to continue. The Permanent Secretary's mouth moved, trying to create the words, and Adrian experienced the usual impulse to help, half forming the words ahead of the other man.

'You're wrong,' Binns finally managed.

Still Adrian said nothing, realizing that Binns had spent a sleepless night trying to justify the suspicions he could not prove. Perhaps, still, the older man wanted the relationship to continue. The hope fluttered momentarily and then died. There was the department to consider, as well, and Adrian had brought that into disrepute.

Binns seized one folder, and from the crimson marking below the 'Strictly Limited' classification Adrian saw it was a collection of reports from the twenty men entrusted with Pavel's safety in Sussex.

'Shall I tell you something about your confident

defector?' said Binns, the sarcasm lost because of the speech difficulty. 'Have you any idea how scared he is?'

'Scared?' queried Adrian.

'Yes, scared. Do you know he refuses to go outside during the day, for exercise, so frightened is he for his own safety. It doesn't even matter that the men prove to him that they are armed.'

'I didn't know that,' said Adrian.

'Always it has to be at night and even then he doesn't allow himself outside the security of the house for longer than fifteen minutes. Being so self-confidently aware of his worth is a two-edged sword as far as Pavel is concerned. He's equally aware of his value to the Russians and how much they'd like to silence him. That man won't have another completely relaxed moment for the rest of his life.'

'So it would seem,' said Adrian. The visit to Binns was unexpected, the demand made in a curt telephone call to his uncomfortable flat by the secretary who could brew Earl Grey tea. Before, reflected Adrian, Binns had made such calls himself. And now there wasn't any tea, either.

'You wanted to see me,' he reminded.

'Yes,' said Binns, discarding the folders. He stopped a yawn with difficulty. 'Something else has arisen.'

'What?'

'We should have anticipated it, of course,' said Binns, refusing to be hurried. 'But I'd overlooked it because of the pressures.'

'What?' repeated Adrian.

'The Russians have officially sought consular access.'

'Oh,' said Adrian. He had thought about it on the first day, a routine move in cases of defection, but, like Binns, had forgotten it.

'It's normal,' said Binns pointlessly.

'I know.'

'The procedure is formulated.'

'I know that, too.' Adrian found himself growing annoyed at the other man's attitude. He'd imagined their friendship deeper than this.

'Pavel will have to be told. The choice whether or not he sees anyone from his own embassy will be entirely his. We must exert no pressure.'

Adrian sighed at the recitation of the standing instructions which had to be learned during the first month in the department. His dismissal really had been decided.

'Do you want me to tell him today?'

'I think so. He should be given every opportunity.'

Adrian smiled at the remark, the sort that Sir William Fornham would have made. Play up, play up and play the game, he mused. Those who cheated were called rotters and those who did what was expected, according to the public school dictum, were jolly good chaps. Adrian thought that the confessions of Kim Philby, whose background the security services had not probed because one gentleman does not question another from the same social stratum, had eradicated such attitudes.

'Make it quite clear,' lectured Binns, 'that the choice is his. If he wants to see his people, then we'll co-operate.'

'He will,' predicted Adrian and Binns looked up, startled.

'What?'

'I said he will,' repeated Adrian.

'What makes you so sure?'

Adrian hesitated. What the hell?

'An impression I have — but one I'm not allowed to consider in my reports,' he said. He immediately regretted it. There was no pleasure in scoring off Binns. If their friendship had died, it was only from one side.

'Humph,' said the older man, upset by Adrian's reaction.

'I suppose,' said Adrian, 'that if Pavel agrees, the meeting will be in the Foreign Office?'

'Yes,' said Binns. 'He'll be brought up overnight, so they won't be able to establish where we're keeping him from the travelling time.'

'When do you want Pavel and Bennovitch brought together?'

'As soon as possible,' said Binns, officiously. 'You heard the P.M. Time's the important thing. That's all that matters now.'

'Do *you* agree? asked Adrian.

'What?'

The question embarrassed the Permanent Secretary.

'Allowing for your disagreement with me over my doubts on Pavel, do you think we should abandon the established routine, one that has shown nearly a hundred per cent success in the past, and hurry the debriefing?'

'It's a special case,' said Binns. 'I think we've got to adjust our handling to suit the circumstances, and the circumstances dictate speed.'

Adrian nodded at the reply, defining Binns's reluctance.

'It's good to know you haven't lost complete faith in me,' he said.

Binns stared at him, but did not reply.

Adrian drove fast, angrily, into Sussex, knowing it was stupid and would achieve nothing, but doing it just the same. He wondered when they'd take the Rover away, with its extra-powerful engine, the car that Anita could never understand their being able to afford, believing his job to be that of a costing accountant at the Ministry of Social Security.

He began creating a mental fact sheet, listing his qualifications for future employment. Age — 35. Height,

5'8". Education — Triple First in modern languages at Oxford, after five years at Eton. Previous experience? — the Official Secrets Act would apply here, so he'd have to hide behind the Social Security lie again, directing any reference inquiries to the department that covered such gaps when a specialized person such as himself was declared no longer employable. Salary expected — minimum of £3,000. Qualifications — none, except the ability to communicate perfectly in twelve different languages and a basic knowledge of psychology. Prospects — nil.

He could try translation, he supposed. Or some job at an airport where his peculiarity might be useful. Or a circus sideshow, he concluded bitterly.

Bennovitch was happy to see him, the truculence of their last meeting completely gone.

'My friend, come back to see me,' he announced, waddling across the room. He seized Adrian's hand, then refused to release him after the greeting, leading him over to the high-backed couch.

'I've missed you,' he said. 'I've looked forward to this day.'

Adrian recalled the whining of three days ago, the complaints of boredom with only Adrian to talk to, and felt his diagnosis of Bennovitch's mental state was being proved more and more by the pendulum of his emotions. He wondered how many years of work the Americans could hope for before Bennovitch had a nervous break-down.

'What news?' asked Bennovitch, the phrase automatic.

Adrian considered the blunt reply. Hadn't the Prime Minister decreed speed? Then he thought of the effect upon Bennovitch's uncertain personality and decided against it.

'When will I see your experts?' asked Bennovitch and then, without waiting for an answer, burbled on, revealing his thoughts of the last two days. 'I have been wondering, will I be allowed any time to meet any American space people?'

Adrian smiled. 'I would think that's pretty inevitable, wouldn't you?'

Bennovitch grinned back, as if they had a secret.

'Are the Americans interested in me?' he asked, anxious for the compliment.

'Very,' replied Adrian.

'And they have got a space programme, which Britain hasn't,' pointed out Bennovitch, as if he were preparing an argument.

Adrian smiled. 'Yes,' he said. 'They have.'

'I went for a walk yesterday, by myself,' Bennovitch declared suddenly, like a child revealing it had learned to count up to ten.

'Really!' encouraged Adrian.

'Yes,' said Bennovitch, pleased that Adrian appeared impressed. 'I told the guards they needn't worry and went down through the meadow and almost to the road ... '

The story trailed away. 'Then I heard some cars and thought I'd better come back.'

From the security officers, with whom he had spoken before meeting Bennovitch, Adrian knew the tiny Russian had stopped a mile from the road and come back almost at a run.

'You must be settling down,' said Adrian.

'I am,' agreed the scientist. 'I'm beginning to feel far more relaxed.'

Adrian felt it was time to start moving towards the point of the meeting.

'Alexandre,' he said, noting the smile the familiarity provoked compared to the annoyance that Pavel had shown. 'I told you when we last met that you'd be meeting our space experts soon. And you will.'

Bennovitch remained smiling.

'But that meeting is being postponed,' Adrian completed, abruptly.

Immediately the attitude of the mercurial Russian changed. He struggled up from the deep couch, his face tight with anger.

'Still you doubt me,' he said. 'Me, Alexandre Gregorovich Bennovitch, one of Russia's leading space scientists. I have co-operated, I have told you all you wanted to know and you treat me like a child ... '

He stopped, searching for invective.

'I go,' he announced. 'I will stay here no longer. America wants me, America can have me. I will go today, now.'

'Alexandre,' soothed Adrian. 'Come back here and sit down.'

'I will not. You are no longer my friend.'

'Alexandre,' repeated Adrian. 'Come here. I have some astonishing news. News that you'll find hard to believe. Come here.'

Suspiciously, Bennovitch came back to the couch and wedged himself in a corner, determined to show his displeasure.

'What?' he said.

Direct or indirect? Adrian juggled the two approaches, uncertain which to employ. What would Ebbetts do? An unnecessary doubt. The Prime Minister would have shown his legendary bluntness within seconds of entering the room. And caused Bennovitch God knows how much mental harm.

Adrian started carefully. 'Tell me,' he said, 'what is your greatest regret at leaving Russia?'

Bennovitch remained suspicious. 'You know. I've already told you.'

'That it means you'll never see Viktor again?'

Bennovitch nodded.

'Had it ever occurred to you that Viktor might think of defecting?'

Adrian suddenly realized that he was conducting the interview in such a way as to support his own doubts. The Prime Minister would hear the tape and recognize it. He shrugged, mentally. So what?

'Viktor, defect!' said Bennovitch. 'Never.'

'Why are you so sure?'

Bennovitch swept out his hand, as if the reasons were too many to list.

'Why should he? He's dedicated, for a start. I think he believes in the system. And he'd gain nothing. I was accorded great honour in my country, but nothing compared to Viktor. His own apartment, chauffeur car, dacha, whatever and whoever he wants in his department ... '

'But he's lost something now that he can't replace. You.'

Bennovitch considered the remark, nodding. 'That's true. We were a team and now that team no longer exists.'

Unexpectedly, Bennovitch disclosed a sudden modesty. 'But Viktor is good by himself,' he said. 'What we were doing will be weakened by our being split, but Viktor is brilliant enough to compensate.'

'But his work *will* suffer,' pressed Adrian. 'It could be that he could feel his work is all-important and worth sacrificing everything for.'

'Ah, you don't know Viktor,' Bennovitch said. 'He's dedicated, I'll agree. And I've never known a more painstaking man, not just with his work, but with everything. But there's one more thing, more important to Viktor than the moon or Mars or space exploration.'

'His family?'

Bennovitch nodded. 'I've never known anyone like Viktor,' said the scientist. 'In the evening, after work was finished, he'd go home and I'd drop by for supper sometimes. There he would be, listening to young Valen-

87

tina play or perhaps there would be a record on. And by his side would be my sister. And do you know what they'd be doing?'

Adrian shook his head.

'Holding hands, like young lovers. They have a special expression for each other. She calls him her best friend: he says she's his dear friend and they say the thing they have between them is deeper than any love and I believe it ... '

He stopped, scrubbing his hand across his eyes, and then went on, 'He can hardly bear to be away from her. Even when she's cooking, he moons around the kitchen, not wanting to be in another room, just watching. A little before I went to Helsinki, when I had made up my mind to defect, I visited the flat. I was actually thinking of telling Viktor, but I decided against it. He was crying and I asked him what was the matter. He smiled and said, "I'm crying in gratitude because I can't believe anyone can be as lucky as I am." And then he said, "Nothing can shatter this happiness." '

Adrian found his concentration slipping. When had he and Anita ever sat alone at home, hand in hand, thinking how lucky they were? When had Anita ever called him a dear friend? When had she uttered anything but abuse, for that matter? 'For Christ's sake, Adrian, why are you such a bloody fool? For Christ's sake, Adrian, why don't you stick up for yourself ... for Christ's sake, Adrian, don't you know people think I'm stupid for marrying you in the first place ... for Christ's sake ... for Christ's sake ... for Christ's sake ... '

He came back to the interview with difficulty.

'It isn't often there is love like that,' agreed Adrian.

'Exactly,' said Bennovitch. 'And Viktor's no fool, believe me. He knows what happens to defectors' families. Leaving them would be like being a judge, sentencing them to jail. Viktor would never do that.'

'Alexandre,' began Adrian and the Russian looked at him, accepting from the tone of his voice that the Englishman was about to say something important.

' ... A little over a week ago, Viktor Pavel slipped away from the Russian delegation at the Paris Air Show and applied for political asylum at our embassy there. He was flown to this country four days ago. I have had a series of interviews with him, which is why our meetings have been interrupted. He has repeated to me his desire to leave Russia and has made an official application to be given asylum in this country.'

Adrian had spoken in a flat monotone, like a public announcement.

Bennovitch looked at him, his pudgy face creased with frowns, shaking his head like a boxer trying to clear his brain after a flurry of punches. Twice he opened his mouth to speak and twice closed it again, unable to translate his thoughts into words.

'No ... it's not ... I can't believe it ... you're lying, trying to trick me. Why are you saying this? I've helped you all I can. Why are you saying this to me?'

'Alexandre, I'm not lying. And I'm not trying to trick you either. Viktor says he had been thinking for some time of defecting ... that he even considered telling *you* but he was not sure of your attitude. He says he was being crushed by the regime and needed room to continue his work in freedom.'

Still Bennovitch shook his head, disbelievingly. 'No. It's not like that ... it's not true ... '

'He's being kept in a country house like this, about twenty miles away ... '

'Then let me see him. Let me meet him, right away. Then I'll believe you. But not until I see him, face to face. Until then, I know you're lying to me.'

'Alexandre, believe me, I'm not. I'll arrange a meeting for you, tomorrow.'

'Tomorrow? I'll see him tomorrow?'

'On my honour.'

The Russian's attitude wavered.

'Oh my God,' he said. 'Poor Valentina ... poor Georgi ... '

The security men guarding Pavel had grown so concerned that they had telephoned London and spoken with Sir Jocelyn. London had got Adrian before he left Bennovitch, and when he arrived at Pulborough, he was given a full briefing. He supposed that Binns would have already told the Premier and that he would be blamed for what had happened. It ceased to matter.

Despite the warning, Adrian was still shocked when he went into the spacious room, overlooking the clipped, tiered lawns, in which the Russian was hunched, as if he were in pain.

Pavel half turned, saw it was Adrian and then looked away again, disinterestedly. His eyes were sore from crying and there were still traces of tears on his face, so white it appeared almost artificially made up.

Although there had been assurances from the security men of room and body searches, Adrian's first thought was that Pavel had taken poison. It had happened once before and security had been as insistent then. The inquiry had shown they'd missed the hollowed-out cross the defector had worn around his neck, a thing they should have checked within the first hour.

'Viktor ... ?'

The Russian ignored him, staring out into the garden.

'Viktor ... what's wrong?'

Adrian moved nearer, going around in front of the other man. He had both hands in front of him and at first Adrian thought he was holding his stomach and that his fear of poison was correct, but then he saw Pavel was clutching the photograph wallet against him, as if he were afraid someone was going to snatch it away.

'Viktor ... tell me. What is it?'

The Russian looked up at him, distress leaking from him. Adrian saw his nose was running and realized he wasn't going to do anything about it. The Englishman felt slightly disgusted.

'Are you ill ... ? Do you want a doctor?'

Pavel shook his head.

'I didn't sleep,' he said.

'I know.'

'I forgot. I'm watched pretty well.'

Adrian said nothing.

'All I could think about was them ... ' He gestured towards the pictures in his lap. 'Do you realize what I've done to them, to my children and my wife?'

Seats had been installed in the bay window of the room: Pavel sat at one end and Adrian sat at the other, studying the man, dismissing his fear of poison.

The breakdown of a man known to adore his wife and family, judged Adrian. A man facing complete realization of the terror he'd left behind. Sincere? Or phoney?

'Do you know what I've done?' repeated Pavel, a man whose mind is blocked by one thought and cannot progress beyond it. 'Do you know they could actually be put to death?'

Adrian nodded, slowly.

'But you knew that, Viktor,' he said, pointedly. There was no reaction at the use of the christian name. 'You must have considered that. It must have been one of the first things that occurred to you.'

Pavel made an uncertain movement.

'Of course I thought about it,' he said. 'But I thought ... Oh, I don't know what I thought ... '

'Really?' queried Adrian. 'That's not like you, Viktor. You're not the sort of man who shuffles a problem aside and hopes some solution will appear, out of the sky.'

The conversation was being recorded, of course. And it would show him to be pressuring a man on the point of collapse. But what if *he* collapsed? Would anyone sympathize about that?

Pavel began crying, quite quietly, just sitting there with tears making tiny rivers down his face. He looked at Adrian, pleadingly.

Adrian felt embarrassed. And guilty. Bullying did not fit him as easily as it did Ebbetts.

'Don't you know what it's like to love someone?' asked Pavel. The sobs edged into his voice.

Yes, thought Adrian. Yes, I know what it's like. And I cried, he remembered.

'But *why* did you defect, Viktor?'

'I told you I'd thought about it for some time,' said Pavel. 'I didn't think I'd really get the exit dossier for Paris. Even when it was granted, I pushed the idea to the back of my mind. It was only in the last day or two that I thought, well, it's now or never. Even in Paris, I was undecided. I thought of Valentina ... of Georgi. And the girl. And then I convinced myself that my reputation would still protect them.'

He looked at Adrian, finally moving his hand across his face. Adrian was glad his nose was clean.

'I was God in Russia,' he said. 'Whatever I said was accepted. I was never questioned or opposed. I thought of what had happened to some of our writers, like Yevtushenko and Solzhenitsyn. They've gone against the regime and stayed in the country and because of the fear of world reaction nothing much has happened to them. I knew my defection would cause a tremendous uproar, especially so close after Alexandre's. I figured that once here, I could give press conferences, make demands and put the spotlight on Moscow, so that no harm would come to my family. I thought that there would be so much publicity about me that the Russians wouldn't be able to make any move against them, put them on trial even. I even day-dreamed that perhaps I'd be able to insist that they come and join me.'

Adrian frowned at the naivety. Perhaps a spoiled man who had had every wish granted for nearly twenty years might think like that, he conceded. Suddenly a flicker of doubt vibrated in his stomach and Adrian realized he could be wrong and that Pavel's defection could be genuine.

'Press conferences could still be arranged,' said Adrian. 'Not yet, but they could be set up.'

Pavel snorted a laugh, dismissing the statement.

'Let's be serious, shall we?' he said. 'Remember how we began our meetings? In complete honesty. I've had nearly eight days to review what I've done. I'm a traitor now, one of the worst there's ever been. They'll do anything, anything to get me. It's insane for me to compare what I've done with what the writers did. And insane, too, to think I can bring any influence against the Soviet Union. Now now. Not any longer. Publicity won't help now. It'll cause more harm, in fact.'

He paused, picking at the photograph. 'They never give up, you know,' he said, quietly. 'They consider abandoning the Soviet Union one of the most serious crimes a Russian can commit. There's actually provision in our criminal statute to try a person who applies for an exit visa to leave permanently.'

Adrian thought of the pressures brought against the Jewish community in Russia in 1970. 'I know,' he said.

'They'll keep on. They'll harm me however they can and they know that the most damaging way would be to hurt my family. They know how much that would hurt me. But even that won't be enough. They'll keep on, for me. Even if it takes years.'

'He'll only go out for exercise at night' — Sir Jocelyn's

words that morning echoed in Adrian's mind. And the doubt about his impressions registered again.

'I was wrong,' said Pavel. 'I've lived in cotton wool for too long. All right, I consider what I do. "The original methodical man" my students used to call me. But I got conceited. I thought that I could do *anything* and not be questioned ... '

He began to cry again. 'What am I going to do?' he sobbed. 'Oh God, what am I going to do?'

For the first time since they had met, three days before, Adrian felt pity for the man.

'I've condemned them to death,' said Pavel. He stared up at Adrian, who saw his nose was running again. 'To death, do you hear me? They're going to die because of me.'

It sounded convincing. Weighed against his conviction that Pavel would not have left his family behind, Adrian admitted to himself that the man's account of why he had crossed to the West sounded genuine. So he *was* wrong.

'Viktor,' he said. 'Your embassy have applied for permission to see you.'

Pavel jerked up, away from the photographs he had been studying again, alarm on his face.

'What is it?' he began, talking quickly. 'What's happened to them? Are they on trial already?'

'Wait,' said Adrian, holding out his hand to stop the runaway fears. 'It's routine in cases of defection. Your people always make a formal application to be allowed to interview their nationals.'

'Why?' Pavel was still suspicious.

'To try and persuade them to go back, of course.'

Pavel sat very quietly for several moments. 'But you'll stop me, of course,' he said.

'Oh no,' said Adrian, quickly. 'If we objected, then we wouldn't have told you of the request, would we?'

Pavel nodded, accepting the honesty.

'Whether or not you see them is entirely for you to decide. If you agree to the meeting, then we'll assist you. It will be in London, at our Foreign Office, and we'll put people with you, if you want us to, so that you'll not be alone during the meeting.'

'Did they ask to see Alexandre?'

'Yes.'

'And what happened?'

'He refused to meet them.'

Pavel smiled, wanly. 'Poor Alexandre. He always was nervous. Not like his sister ... '

His voice broke at the reminiscence.

'Will they threaten me?' he asked, suddenly.

'Probably,' said Adrian, honestly.

'Will they tell me what's happened to Valentina and the children?'

Adrian shrugged. 'I can't answer that, can I?'

'No, of course not. I'm sorry.'

Pavel lapsed into silence and Adrian looked beyond him, over the lawns which descended in steps to the river which formed a barrier at the back of the house. With fishing rights at about £150 a rod, the Home Office were losing a fortune closing off this much ground, he thought.

Pavel was sitting with his head drooping forward on his chest, breathing deeply. So quiet was he that at one stage Adrian suspected he had fallen asleep through the exhaustion of staying awake the previous night and he actually bent forward, until he could see that Pavel's eyes were open. He was staring, almost unblinkingly, at the pictures. It was nearly thirty minutes before Pavel spoke and when he snapped up, suddenly, there was just a trace of the command which had been so evident at their earlier meetings.

'I want to see them,' he announced.

Expecting the decision, Adrian nodded.

'How soon could it be arranged?' asked the Russian.

'Tomorrow morning,' replied Adrian. 'We'd thought that some time tomorrow you could meet Alexandre, too.'

Pavel smiled, suddenly, at the invitation.

'Alexandre,' he said. 'Yes, that would be good.'

The smile disappeared. 'But I want to see the embassy people before tomorrow morning.'

'But that's not possible,' protested Adrian.

'Why not?' queried Pavel, looking at his watch. 'It's only two-thirty. What's wrong with this evening? Are their dinners more important than me, Viktor Pavel?'

The recovery improves by the minute, thought Adrian. He said, 'That's not it. You've got to be taken to London ... '

'If it only took an hour by helicopter from Brussels to England, it can't take longer to get to London by the same transport, unless we're in the far reaches of Scotland and I know we're not.'

Adrian smiled. 'No,' he admitted, 'we're not in Scotland.'

'I want to meet them tonight,' insisted Pavel. 'I can't stand another night like I had last night. I must know. They must tell me what's happening to my family.'

'The man you meet won't know that,' warned Adrian.

'He might.'

'I know these meetings,' said Adrian. 'They're almost as routine as the initial request.'

'I don't care,' rejected Pavel, his customary annoyance at being challenged emerging. 'He *might* know and that's good enough for me.'

'I still don't know whether it's possible,' said Adrian.

'But there are telephones. Try. It must be tonight.'

A helicopter did nullify Binns's fears of the Russians assessing the debriefing spot from travelling time, admitted Adrian. And according to Ebbetts, speed was the major consideration for everything.

'I'll see,' he promised, getting up from the padded seat.

As Adrian left the room, Pavel was staring back at the picture, and he recalled leaving Bennovitch in a similar window-nook three days before, in an identical position, gazing down at another photograph. Everyone carries reminders, thought Adrian. I wonder if Anita has a portrait to remind her of me? No, he decided. If she had any pictures at all, they wouldn't be for nostalgic reminders. Just for amusement among her new friends.

Kaganov made a tiny tower with his hands and tilted his chair back on two legs. He smiled, a man knowing inner contentment.

'That was quick,' he said.

'What happened?' asked Minevsky.

'We got a reply within eight hours of making the request for access,' said the chairman.

Heirar frowned. 'Only eight hours. I expected to wait at least two days.'

'So did I,' said Kaganov. 'So did I.'

Minevsky chuckled, preparing the others for the joke.

'You haven't told us what the answer was,' he said.

Kaganov joined in the laughter. 'Forgive me,' he said. 'Pavel wants to meet someone from the embassy. And he wants the meeting tonight.'

'There!' said Minevsky, in heavy irony. 'Perhaps he doesn't like England after all.'

Heirar waited for the amusement to subside, and then said, 'What about Pavel's son?'

'Georgi?' queried Kaganov. 'He's at Alma Ata. You knew that.'

He had forgotten. 'We haven't moved him yet, then?' said Heirar, trying to recover.

'Oh no,' said Kaganov. 'Not yet.'

97

Chapter Eight

Adrian travelled with Pavel in a chauffeur-driven car, leaving his own vehicle at Pulborough for collection the following day. They went a roundabout route, going east into Kent and then looping back, approaching London from the Maidstone direction.

It was a bright, sharp night, the stars set into the sky like jewelled buttons.

Pavel slumped in the seat alongside Adrian, staring up.

'Hundreds of millions of miles away,' he said softly. 'Look at them. Some we know about, some we don't. They just glitter there, the winning posts for a race of giants. I wonder if it really matters who gets there first. Or whether anybody gets there at all.'

'That's an odd doubt, coming from someone like you,' said Adrian.

Pavel looked at him in the darkened car. 'Why?' he asked. 'I just make it possible. I don't say whether it should be done.'

He twisted, looking out through the darkened rear window.

'Are we alone?'

Adrian remembered his nervousness. 'No,' he said, 'of course not. There are two cars, one in front, one behind. There's no risk.'

'Very professional,' said Pavel. 'I can't make out either of them.'

'They wouldn't be much good, if you could, would they?' remarked Adrian, mildly. He felt hungry and wondered if the canteen would be open when they arrived. Probably not. But there was always that French restaurant near the B.O.A.C. terminal at Victoria. He'd taken Anita there on one of their first dates, trying to impress her with his worldliness, insisting on ordering the meal and the wine in French, like an A-level schoolboy. No, not quite like an A-level schoolboy. His accent was better. Yes, La Bicyclette would be nice. He'd go there, even if the canteen were open. A French meal and a bottle of wine and a headache in the morning and damn them all. In his mind he parodied Ebbetts's hectoring tones: 'The condemned man ate a hearty meal, took the bill to put on his expenses and even had a brandy.' He might even have two brandies.

He looked at the dashboard clock glowing ahead of him. They'd be in that comfortable flat now, overlooking the Thames and they'd be drinking brandy, too, Anne probably holding her glass out, registering her dominance, Anita fluttering from the drinks trolley, eager to please, like a newly wed housewife. He paused at the thought. I suppose she is, really, he decided.

'Will we come back tonight?'

Adrian jumped. 'What?'

'Will we come back tonight?' repeated the Russian.

'No. It's already arranged. We'll stay in London and then travel down to see Alexandre tomorrow.'

He hesitated, then added, 'We've decided to take your advice. Tomorrow we'll travel by helicopter. We decided there was enough time to use the car tonight.'

It had been Adrian's idea, when he realized that to stay overnight would mean travelling back in daylight, with more chance of detection.

They arrived in London just before eleven and Adrian's intention to have a French meal collapsed with the summons to see Binns in his office. It had been decided that Adrian should not attend the interview with Pavel, although the Russian had demanded that he be accompanied.

The risk of a British debriefing expert, even one about to be fired, being recognized and marked by a member of the Russian embassy had to be avoided.

The Permanent Secretary nodded curtly and indicated his usual chair and Adrian realized his dismissal had not been reconsidered.

'Not a very edifying meeting this afternoon, was it?' he said, the stutter jerking the words from him.

'No,' agreed Adrian.

'We detected little sympathy in some of your remarks.'

Adrian noted the 'we'. So Binns had listened with the Prime Minister and others.

'I wasn't aware I was employed to show sympathy,' retorted Adrian, disregarding the usual respect. Why the hell should he sit and take criticism from everyone? His thoughts stopped. Why the hell? — that phrase wouldn't have come to mind a few days ago. But then, neither would the thought of getting drunk on French wine and brandy have appealed, either.

'I thought the only need was speed: milk the man dry and then play international politics with him and Bennovitch, like disposable chess pieces.'

Binns noticeably winced. Adrian realized that the gap between them was widening at every meeting.

'That is the point,' agreed the Permanent Secretary, trying to compete. 'But you don't seem to be achieving it. What was the result of today's meeting? Nothing.'

'I acted today under instructions,' snapped Adrian. He was reddening and stumbling over his words, but curiously, like a man getting drunk for the first time, he found himself enjoying anger. He didn't have to worry about conforming any more. There was no feeling of sickness now or the need to go to the lavatory.

Not yet, anyway.

'On *your* instructions,' he continued, his voice rising. 'I told Pavel of the request of his embassy. At *your* request, I gave him every assistance and he wanted to come immediately, which is why I phoned you from Pulborough and set it up, and why there was no debriefing today. It's not *my* way of conducting the debriefing.'

Binns was sitting with his head lowered and for a long time he did not respond. When he looked up, his face was twisted, as if he were in physical pain.

'It's split us up, this thing, hasn't it?' he asked, not needing an answer. 'In less than a week, we've become enemies almost. And we were friends. We had a mutual respect that went beyond the job, but now we're people on either side of a fence. I never thought that would happen.'

He stopped, for a moment. Then he said, 'That's bad, very bad.'

He sounded extremely sad.

Adrian's truculence disappeared. He felt embarrassed.

'I'm sorry, too,' he said and meant it. He wished he could have put it better.

'I argued against your dismissal,' said Binns. 'No one, no team such as we were can gauge every situation. You've brought out nearly everything with Bennovitch and I'm sure, in the end, it would have been a complete debriefing, with nothing undisclosed. You've achieved quite a lot with Pavel. I made the points, as strongly as I could, to the P.M.'

Adrian noted that the impediment had disappeared. Was it possible to recross broken bridges?

'But then there was the meeting … ' went on Binns.

' … and I opposed him,' finished Adrian. 'I was impertinent and unconvincing and made myself look stupid. But surely if I'm right, then he'll admit he's wrong?'

Binns laughed aloud, a rare thing, and Adrian noticed a lot of his teeth were bad. Perhaps he was frightened of the dentist.

'Oh,' said Adrian, accepting the unspoken contradiction. Secretly he still hoped for the miracle, the sudden move that would prove his doubts were correct, even though he was now unsure about them. Now, it seemed, it wouldn't matter. Ebbetts was never wrong. Never.

'I see Pavel asked to be accompanied,' said Binns.

Adrian nodded. 'We'll get a full report by morning,' he said. 'I know the two men with him.'

'What do you think?'

Adrian looked at the man who had been his friend for fifteen years. If he were to preserve his integrity, he had to be honest.

'I think I was wrong,' he said.

Binns jerked up, faced with an answer he hadn't expected.

'I didn't ... ' he began and stopped.

'I believed there was something wrong about Pavel's defection,' continued Adrian. 'I still do. It's still too illogical for a man like that. But he's genuine about his family. I spent six hours with that man today. I've never seen anyone more sincerely torn apart by fear of what is going to happen to his wife and children than he is.'

Binns stared at him. 'Where does that leave you and your suspicions?' he asked, finally.

Adrian felt tears coming and fought them, coughing repeatedly to explain the way he spoke.

'God only knows,' he admitted. 'Perhaps I'm wrong. Perhaps I'm wrong and Ebbetts is right and I deserve to be replaced because I'm no longer any good.'

Binns looked away, recognizing the emotion and wanting to spare his assistant. What the hell do men come into this business for, he thought. But Adrian had changed his mind. His doubts were wavering and that was a factor to be considered and so he'd have to tell the Prime Minister. But not now, not tonight. He could wait until the morning. It wouldn't make any difference now.

'By the way,' said Binns. 'There's been a complaint.'

Adrian looked at him curiously.

'The maintenance department,' continued the Permanent Secretary. 'They say you've defaced the window-sill of your office.'

'It's chocolate,' said Adrian.

'Chocolate?'

'There was a pigeon. I put chocolate biscuits out for it.'

'Oh.'

'It won't happen again,' promised Adrian. 'The pigeon's gone away.'

Chapter Nine

Pavel had been lodged overnight in north London, in a large house on the outskirts of Islington. Adrian collected him at nine and in the back of the curtained Rover they went out along Western Avenue towards Northolt, where the helicopter was waiting.

Pavel said nothing.

He hadn't even spoken when Adrian got to Islington, just given a brief nod of recognition and then allowed himself to be hurried into the vehicle, a man completely resigned to being moved from one spot to another at the will of others. There was no fight in him now, no arrogance or conceit. He was completely drained of everything, everything except his secrets.

Adrian had been to the office early, studying with Binns the reports of the two men who had attended the meeting between the embassy official and Pavel.

It was a lengthy, twenty-page typescript, sectioned into question and answer. Adrian read it twice, the second time analysing it sentence by sentence, briefing himself for the later meeting with the scientist.

Binns had sighed, throwing his copy on the desk.

'What do you think?'

'Brilliant,' Adrian had judged, immediately.

'Brilliant?'

'I don't think I've ever seen a document where one man has so successfully left another with a greater sense of his own guilt. That man isn't just an official at their embassy. He's a psychiatrist. And a good one.'

'That's exactly what I felt,' Binns had replied.

Adrian had experienced a stir of pleasure, knowing that they'd reached the same conclusion.

Binns had continued, 'It was wrong exposing Pavel to that interview, if we want to keep him.'

'You know how I felt about that. And that the meeting with Bennovitch should be postponed,' Adrian had warned, urgently. 'If Pavel, after last night, is thrown together with Bennovitch, then it'll be another day wasted.'

'I know. I've already warned the P.M. I said just that.'

'And?'

'He's ordered that the meeting go ahead.'

Adrian had sighed. And he'd be blamed. Whatever went wrong, Ebbetts had already established the scape-goat, the sacrifice to defeat if defeat occurred.

Adrian had anticipated the mood that Pavel would be in, but the depth of remorse and despair surprised him.

Adrian, who had visited the British embassy in Moscow and knew the city, smiled out of the car and tried small talk.

'The English traffic,' he said. 'Different from what you're used to.'

Pavel didn't even bother to grunt a response.

'We're going to see Alexandre,' Adrian persisted. 'It won't take long, by helicopter.'

The car cleared Wembley and picked up speed along the dual carriageway. Adrian relaxed, relieved that the car, an ideal target in the slow-moving traffic, was no longer so vulnerable.

'Alexandre is looking forward to it,' he pressed on, trying to break down the barrier.

Slowly Pavel turned to him. He'd stopped crying so much, but his complexion was grey and putty-like. If I touched his face, thought Adrian, the finger-mark would stay.

'He wouldn't tell me,' said Pavel. His voice was flat and unsure, like a man speaking for the first time after a long illness. 'I asked him. I kept on asking him and then I pleaded and he looked at me and his face didn't move, not at all. He just shrugged.'

Adrian didn't reply. He'd seen the typescript, the incessant question from the defector repeated over and over again: 'My family. What's happened to my family?'

Adrian expected tears, but Pavel seemed to have progressed beyond that now. He sat in the far corner of the car.

'They've arrested them, haven't they? They've arrested them and put them on trial. They're going to die. They're going to die because of what I've done. I've killed them.'

Adrian sensed the growing hysteria and spoke quickly, anxious to halt it.

'Stop it, Viktor. We don't know that. You're guessing.'

'I don't have to guess. I know.'

They paused at the gate to the R.A.F. station, identified themselves and then swept into the restricted section, where the Westland Whirlwind waited under guard.

Again, moving like someone mentally retarded, entirely dependent on others, Pavel was led from the car, seated and belted into the helicopter and then obediently lowered his head, while the flight sergeant fumbled with the regulation helmet. Adrian had to wear one, too, and sat in the machine feeling stupid and self-conscious.

The protection prevented conversation and so they sat side by side in the helicopter, just looking down. To prevent Pavel knowing where he was being taken, the helicopter flew directly west, down to Dorset, over the neat fields set out like a giant stamp collection, before turning south out over the Channel, so there were no landmarks, and then retracing its route to the east. It crossed the coast again at Hastings and looped Pulborough to where Bennovitch was being held.

Pavel struggled from the machine, hobbling with cramp and for the first time Adrian realized how old he was. Fifty-nine, thought Adrian. Fifty-nine and just five days ago he seemed ageless. Now he looked like a senile old man.

He stood waiting for instructions beneath the helicopter, which drooped, like a huge insect caught in the rain.

Adrian put an arm around his shoulders and gently propelled him towards the house. The Russian approached docilely, without comment. Adrian felt he would have walked just as unquestioningly away from the house if he had been ordered to, so little interest was he taking in what happened to him.

As they got nearer, Adrian isolated the elegant room where all his debriefings with the other Russian had taken place and then he saw Bennovitch, his head barely above the window-sill. He was standing quite motionless, still not completely convinced that it was Pavel who was being brought to him.

When they were very close, Bennovitch's face cleared and a half smile formed. He tried a hesitant wave, shyly almost, as if he expected to be rejected for what he had done. Pavel made no response and Bennovitch's face settled into a frown of uncertainty.

Adrian touched the older Russian's arm, then gestured towards the window. Pavel's eyes focused and Bennovitch saw he had been recognized and he smiled again, more hopefully this time.

Adrian glanced back to his companion, like a father encouraging a reluctant son to acknowledge a birthday aunt. And remained staring at Pavel. Never had he seen such a look of sadness on a man's face. The look lasted a few seconds, then faded.

They hurried in and Bennovitch burst into the hall before Pavel could take off his light Russian-style summer raincoat. They both stood there, in the high-ceilinged, timbered hall, with its wide, baronial stairway lined with shields and swords of forgotten battles, just looking at each other.

No one spoke and Adrian became aware of the slow, sticky tick of the grandfather clock near the beginning of the stairs. It sounds like an old man's heart, he thought, weak and at any moment ready to stop bothering. He waited, expecting the noise to cease, but it went on, monotonously.

Bennovitch moved first, very slowly, raising his arms as he walked and then Pavel started forward and they fell into each other's embrace, the traditional Russian greeting, kissing each other repeatedly on the cheek. Still they said nothing. Adrian saw both were crying.

Finally Pavel held the smaller man at arm's length, studying him.

'Alexandre,' he mouthed, softly.

'Viktor.'

They hugged each other again and then Bennovitch turned, leading the other man back into the beautiful room with its view of the garden. Pavel kept his arm around Bennovitch's shoulders protectively, and neither seemed aware that Adrian had followed them into the room.

They went to a long couch drawn up before the open, dead fireplace, the hearth disguised by horse-chestnut branches cut from the grounds. Adrian edged into an armchair and sat, waiting.

Pavel spoke first and when he did it was in the dull monotone of the car ride to the airfield.

'He wouldn't tell me,' he said, searching Bennovitch's face as if the other man would have an explanation for the diplomat's refusal. 'I asked him, again and again, but he wouldn't reply.'

Bennovitch sat motionless, his face ridged in puzzlement. This was not the man he knew, the autocratic, overbearing genius he'd left six weeks before in a massive Moscow laboratory where the technicians jumped at his very presence. This was not the Hero of the Soviet Union, the holder of more awards than any other Russian civilian, the man to whom the scientists of the world looked in awe.

This was a rambling old man.

Adrian thought Bennovitch looked disappointed and suddenly he recognized the parallel. He and Binns. Pavel and Bennovitch. Disappointment? Yes, certainly that, but there was more. Each—Binns in him perhaps, certainly Bennovitch in Pavel—had created an ideal, an image without any flaws.

But now the picture was blurred.

A man had become superman and there was no such thing. Men were just men and women were just women. He paused, thinking of Anita. Well, almost always.

Sir Jocelyn had realized it and now he stuttered when they met. Bennovitch was baffled and now he stared in disbelief.

Sad, decided Adrian. It was a pity people couldn't keep the perfection they had imagined rather than having to accept reality. It was like shopping in a street market. People always expected a bargain and always got second best.

'Viktor,' tried Bennovitch. 'What is it?'

Pavel looked at his assistant.

'He wouldn't tell me,' he repeated, stupidly.

Adrian had wanted to remain outside their thoughts, hoping they wouldn't even notice his presence. But now he realized that unless he prompted the conversation the two men would spend their meeting in near-silence.

'Alexandre,' he said, quietly, introducing himself almost. 'Viktor met an official from your embassy last night.'

The uncertainty lifted from Bennovitch's face and he turned to the other Russian.

'You shouldn't have done it, Viktor. You should have kept away.'

Pavel looked at him, the deadness slipping away from his face.

'But Valentina. What about Valentina? And the children.'

Bennovitch nibbled at his fingers. 'Do you think I haven't considered that?' he said.

Adrian relaxed, realizing the dam in the conversation had been breached.

'When I left, it didn't matter, because you were there and they wouldn't consider any move. But now ... '

Bennovitch stumbled to a halt, unable to express himself.

'They'll face trial,' said Pavel, positively. 'They'll torture me, by proxy.'

'And me.'

For a moment, there was silence. Then Bennovitch said, 'My poor sister.'

'My poor wife.'

'Then why?'

The question burst from Bennovitch, suddenly freed from the hero worship and the restrictions under which he had worked for fifteen years. There was no anger from Pavel at the abrupt demand from his assistant.

'I was wrong,' he admitted. 'Oh, I was so wrong.' He stopped, gazing at the floor, embarrassed almost to meet the look of the other man.

'I was worried about the experiments, about the Mars probe and the space platform. It was getting more and more restrictive. I was thinking of defecting months ago ...'

He paused, smiling for the first time.

'Funny,' he said, 'I told myself that if I went, then your position would protect Valentina and the children until I could get them out. But you went first from the Helsinki conference ...'

Now it was the turn of Bennovitch to appear embarrassed, as if he owed an explanation.

'I'm sorry,' he said.

'I never knew,' said Pavel, in another aside, 'I never guessed you were thinking of going over.'

Bennovitch grinned at him, glad they shared a secret. 'Neither did I of you. And I thought I knew you so well.'

Pavel shrugged. 'Anyway, once you'd gone, there was tremendous pressure. The whole department came under the most fantastic investigation I've ever known. It was far worse than anything that happened under Stalin. Everyone was checked and then checked again ... '

He hesitated again. 'God knows what it will be like now,' he said.

He went on. 'I was hauled before the inner committee ... '

'Kaganov?' interrupted Bennovitch. There was fear etched into the question.

Pavel nodded. 'I got the whole lecture. The demands for dossier files on all my staff, everything like that. I had to agree to the employment of two political commissars, actually in the laboratory. And then they told me that the budget would be cut back. I had proved politically unreliable and therefore the work had to come to a standstill until the department had cleared itself of any involvement.'

'You?' Bennovitch seemed incredulous. 'They imposed restrictions on you?'

Pavel nodded. 'Kaganov seemed to enjoy it. He even quoted a Western axiom to me. "No one is indispensable," he told me. "Not even you." '

Bennovitch shook his head in disbelief and Pavel smiled at him.

'You've no idea of the problems you caused. I was in complete turmoil. You, someone I loved like a brother, had defected. The work in the department was blocked for six months, maybe longer. I wasn't thinking straight, I thought I was important, more important than I was. I convinced myself that once out, I could get the family out as well. Now I realize that isn't possible.'

'What did he say last night?'

Pavel didn't reply immediately. He sat, recalling the conversation with the diplomat.

'Just that I should come back. That I had disgraced the Soviet Union, but that they were prepared to forgive me and let me go back.'

'Do you believe them?'

Pavel considered the question, then grimaced, without replying.

'I wouldn't see them,' announced Bennovitch, as if the refusal indicated bravery. 'The English were very fair, they said it was entirely my choice and I decided there was no point.'

Both men, who were speaking in Russian, appeared to have forgotten Adrian was in the room.

'But I had to know,' protested Pavel, picking up the familiar theme. 'I had to try and find out what had happened to them.'

Silence settled again and Adrian was afraid they had reached another barrier. He sat, reluctant to intrude.

Then Bennovitch asked, suddenly, 'How has the work gone?'

'Well,' said Pavel. 'Most of it stopped immediately you left, of course. We began working on the calculations you'd made about flight adjustments after launch. Remember, we didn't spend much time on them. But the unmanned Mars probe was sending back interesting data. Do you know it recorded solar wind speeds of 350 miles a second?'

'That fast! But that will create just the adjustment difficulties I foresaw.'

'I know. Do you realize how much more important

that made your defection? Let me tell you what I considered.'

Pavel took paper from his pocket and began writing formulae and suddenly the age and indecision and self-pity lifted from him. A change came over Bennovitch, too. The nervousness ceased as he immersed himself in what Pavel was saying, occasionally querying a fact or a calculation. Adrian looked on fascinated as the two men worked, appreciating for the first time how necessary one was to the other. Apart, they were two brilliant scientists, their space knowledge and ideas far beyond those of any Western counterpart. Together they were spectacular, each grasping the idea of the other before the sentence was completely uttered, two men wholly in tune with each other. Like twins, thought Adrian, twins sharing between them an incomparable brain.

Suddenly he saw their incredible importance. And realized too, how far ahead Ebbetts was planning to use that importance. Adrian felt admiration for the Prime Minister and then immediately begrudged the feeling. Always right. The politicians were always right and by the time the memoirs were written, the excuses had been established.

The door opened at the far end of the long room and one of the security officers entered.

The two Russians stared at him and momentarily Pavel's face clouded, as if he had forgotten where he was and was about to rebuke a worker for intruding into a laboratory where a vital conference was being held.

Then Adrian said, 'Thank you,' and they were both reminded of him and the mood was broken.

'I'm being taken away?'

There was surprise in Pavel's question.

'For a while ... ' began Adrian, but then Bennovitch cut in. 'But this is ridiculous. Madness. Why should we be parted?'

'Because we have decided it should be so,' replied Adrian, abruptly. The authority had to be maintained.

'Oh,' said Bennovitch, punctured.

'From one master to another,' said Pavel and there was a hint of the mockery of their first meetings.

'Come now, Viktor,' replied Adrian, mocking too, 'That's not so and you know it.'

Pavel smiled and said, 'Yes. Yes I know it,' and the remark registered. It was the first time Pavel had conceded that what he had found might be better than what he had left behind. An improvement, judged Adrian. Very slight, but an improvement.

'We've got to go to the other house,' he said, an unnecessary explanation. 'We will probably decide to put you together by the end of the week.'

Pavel and Bennovitch looked at each other and then back at Adrian, resigned.

'We'll meet tomorrow?' Bennovitch asked Adrian. The Englishman nodded.

'Good,' said the tiny Russian.

The windows of the car in which they returned to Pulborough were completely blackened and then curtained. Pavel smiled at the protection.

'You make me think I'm valuable.'

'I don't have to tell you that. You know your value,' replied Adrian. He was happy that the Russian thought the protection was for his benefit.

'How was it, meeting Alexandre again?' asked Adrian.

The Russian thought about the question.

'Good,' he said, inadequately. 'It was good to see him.'

'The work won't be interrupted,' offered Adrian, hopefully, trying to reinforce the other man's decision to defect. 'In two months, maybe less, you could be in your own laboratory again, working at just the same degree of experimentation as you were before.'

Pavel ignored the encouragement. He closed his eyes

against the pale interior light of the car and was silent for a long time.

Then he said, 'Valentina, oh God, Valentina,' and Adrian realized that the whole day had been wasted.

'It took place,' reported Kaganov.

'What happened?' Minevsky managed the question just ahead of Heirar.

'Just what we expected,' continued the chairman. 'He could talk of nothing except his wife and family. London say he asked at least ten times.'

'They didn't answer, of course,' anticipated Heirar, safely.

'Of course not,' agreed Kaganov.

'What about the boy?' asked Minevsky, suddenly reminded. 'Are we still keeping him down on the border?'

'No,' dismissed Kaganov. 'That brat is important. He's being moved tomorrow. We've got to show we're serious.'

' "Men of our word", as the British might say,' quoted Heirar, amused at his own joke.

'Always that,' laughed Kaganov. 'Always men of our word.'

Chapter Ten

Adrian had been in the office for forty-five minutes before Miss Aimes arrived. Momentarily, she seemed startled to find him there, her hand darting up to her head, as if the coiffure might have slipped.

'I didn't think you were coming in today,' she said and then stopped, aware she was revealing a weakness.

'There were things to do,' said Adrian. He stopped, uncertain. Then he added, 'Things I haven't been able to do because you weren't here.'

They stared at each other in complete silence. It felt good, very good. Adrian sat at his desk, on his trouser-protecting pad with his pen-and-pencil tray like a demarcation line between them, warmed by the feeling. He should have done it ages ago, prevented her attitude getting as bad as it had, but now he'd stopped it. Now he was imposing his authority and he enjoyed the experience. Yes, it was very good.

'I came back last night,' he pressed on. 'But the office was empty, thirty minutes before it should have been, otherwise I could have warned you I wanted to make a prompt start. I had ... '

He stopped, enjoying his suddenly discovered hardness. Did Ebbetts feel like this that day in the small office off the Cabinet Room when he had imposed his will? Is this how powerful men felt, subjugating the weak?

'I *had*,' he picked up again, emphasizing the irony, 'hoped we could have done everything in this first hour.'

He halted again, taken by a sudden thought. He'd ask

her ... no, not ask, he'd tell her she had to work late. He'd demand that she stay until he returned from the second day's meeting between Pavel and Bennovitch and clear the backlog that had accumulated. There was a lot to be done, several days' work in fact, but it didn't matter. After all, he had nowhere to go, that evening or any other.

Today Jessica Emily Aimes, spinster, fifty-three, of Ash Drive, Bromley, Kent, was going to be put in her place. He'd crush her truculence and her bossy attitude and for his few remaining days in the department enjoy a proper relationship with the woman.

Christ, how she'd hate working late.

'So ... ' he began, enjoying the build-up, 'I'd like you to ... '

'Your wife rang.'

She cut him off decisively, a person who had waited for her moment of interruption to achieve the maximum impact.

'What?'

'Your wife rang.' She allowed a momentary pause, while her eyes swept the unpressed suit and grubby shoes. 'I asked her how her mother was, you having told me how unwell the poor lady was and how your wife had to go to the country to care for her ... '

Another pause, for a staged smile of uncertainty.

'She didn't seem to know what I was talking about,' she completed.

Adrian hunched behind the pen-and-pencil set, head turned towards the empty window, to avoid her direct stare. Despite their complaints, the maintenance people hadn't cleaned the window-sill and the chocolate was parched, like a dried-up riverbed. It wouldn't be today, not now. Today she'd won. Again. Perhaps tomorrow.

'What did she want?'

'She asked me to give you the address of a solicitor,'

said Miss Aimes and again there was that smirk. She handed him a piece of paper. Runthorpe, Golding and Chapel, Pauls Mews, London EC2. Very respectable-sounding, he thought. I wonder how many lesbians Mr Runthorpe had acted for in the past? Still, who said it was a man? Perhaps it was a Miss Runthorpe, all part of Anita's new set of friends.

'You wanted to ask me something?'

Adrian looked at her, puzzled. 'What?'

'You were complaining of my being late and going to ask me something,' reminded Miss Aimes, confidently.

'Oh, it was nothing,' said Adrian. 'Nothing at all. We'll talk about it tomorrow.'

Miss Aimes wouldn't let go.

'Are you sure?'

'Yes,' said Adrian, 'quite sure.'

They reversed the routine the second day, bringing Bennovitch across country to Pulborough. Pavel had seemed surprised, at first, as if expecting to go to the other man, but then he accepted the change without comment. The scientist was withdrawn, grunting reactions to Adrian's attempts at conversation while they awaited the other Russian.

Bennovitch waddled in, like a newborn bear on show at a zoo for the first time. Adrian noticed that the nervousness was subdued, the hands not automatically in his mouth now.

As before, the two men embraced and immediately began talking.

'I've worked on the solar wind speeds, during the night. Look.'

Bennovitch produced his calculations proudly, anticipating praise. Adrian remembered the jottings of the previous day. What had happened to them? A mistake, he realized. He'd have to collect them. Had Pavel taken them? He couldn't remember.

The two men launched into a technical discussion of calculations. And in Russian, mused Adrian. That would take some translation and analysis. But that didn't matter. Ebbetts was getting what he wanted, the information that the two men possessed, and in two weeks' time he'd initiate his diplomacy and get something from every side.

But the major benefit would be for Ebbetts and Britain. That, supposed Adrian, was the meaning of statesmanship, the successful manipulation of everybody and every country and everything to your own advantage.

He wondered if statesmen and prime ministers and diplomats ever regretted afterwards the concessions and compromises and ruthlessness necessary to earn their reputations. Probably not. The end always justifies the means, unless the end deviates from the expected success, and then the inbuilt protection is brought forth, and the mistakes can be shown as those of others.

Life, thought Adrian, the sort of life he lived, was a shit. Everyone was a shit, him and the people he dealt with and even the things he had to do. A shit.

He sat, half listening to the two Russians, enjoying the description. Everything was certainly changing. That was a word that would not have presented itself three weeks before. Adrian Dodds, you're growing up. He sighed. Growing up. But too late. A shit. He brought the word to mind again, consciously, enjoying his mental graffito, like a fourteen-year-old inscribing his adulthood on a lavatory wall. But my way is safer than lavatory walls, thought Adrian. I can't get caught.

Pavel was nodding, accepting Bennovitch's argument, and the younger man was smiling shyly. If he had a tail, thought Adrian, he'd wag it.

The Englishman suddenly became conscious that they

were recognizing his presence in the room and began to concentrate.

'I asked you a question,' said Bennovitch testily, eager to prove his attitude towards the interrogator.

Adrian smiled. There was no point in constantly defeating the tiny man.

'I'm sorry,' he said, deferentially. 'What did you say?'

'When will we be allowed to be together all the time?'

'Soon,' said Adrian, vaguely. 'It's pointless occupying two houses. It's obviously better for you to be together. I'll make the recommendation tonight.'

'And the debriefing takes so much less time, doesn't it?'

The cynicism of three days before emerged unexpectedly and Adrian looked at Pavel.

'Yes,' he conceded, 'so much less time.'

'We'll go to America, won't we?' asked Bennovitch. He seemed anxious to prove himself constantly to the other Russian. A son with an inferiority complex trying to compete with a brilliant father, decided Adrian.

'That depends.' He began to hedge, but Pavel intruded, abruptly.

'Oh no it doesn't,' he contradicted. 'What use would we have in Britain, whose space programme is limited to a firework on the Woomera rocket range?'

You'd be surprised, thought Adrian. He smiled at Pavel. 'Of course America wants you,' he said. 'You don't need me to tell you that. Washington has officially asked that their embassy here be given access to you as soon as possible. They intend making you an offer, obviously. And it'll be a good one.'

'Sought after,' mocked Pavel, speaking to the other Russian. 'We're being fought over, Alexandre.'

Bennovitch misunderstood the irony and smiled happily, pleased that they were being considered together, each as useful as the other. A year, judged Adrian, perhaps eighteen months at the outside before Benno-vitch had a breakdown.

One of the security men entered and nodded and Pavel said, still sarcastic, 'Visiting time is up. Time to go.'

Bennovitch looked from him to Adrian and then back again, trying to gauge the feeling that existed between them and failing.

Adrian nodded to Bennovitch. 'It's time to go, Alex-andre,' he said. 'You've been here three hours.'

'Tomorrow?' asked the younger Russian.

'Of course. Perhaps for good.'

Bennovitch smiled and turned back to Pavel. They embraced again and as Bennovitch began to move back Pavel held him, the affection almost embarrassing.

Adrian sat unspeaking with Pavel for several moments after Bennovitch had gone. He felt unsettled. He couldn't isolate the cause or harden the feeling beyond a vague impression. And he wasn't allowed impressions any more, by direct order from the Prime Minister.

'You have a lot, haven't you?' said Pavel.

'What?'

'I can tell by the freedom with which Alexandre talks that he's told you a lot.'

'He's been helpful,' allowed Adrian, guardedly.

'And with us together, it's one hundred times better, isn't it?'

'You seem to be a fantastic team,' admitted Adrian.

'We are,' said Pavel, without conceit, 'we are.'

Silence settled again. The feeling persisted in Adrian. Pavel stood up, wandering without direction around the room, and Adrian was reminded of an actor rehearsing his lines. When Pavel sat down, it proved an apt simile.

'I don't want to see Alexandre again,' he began.

So his impression had been right. That was his imme-diate reaction, the knowledge that he was going to be proved right. He had warned of something unusual

happening and here it was. Adrian wondered what
Ebbetts's response would be.

'What?'

'I said I don't want to see Alexandre any more.'

'But why ... ?' Adrian forced the question, aware of
the answer.

Pavel got up and completed another tour of the room
before he answered. Then, spacing the words as if anxious
there should be no misunderstanding, he said, 'I want to
go back.'

Adrian stared at him. He'd known the unexpected
would happen, told them even. It had been an impression
and now it was a fact. It had to be stretched, explored to
the fullest degree. Ebbetts had to know how accurate
his assessment had been. That's vanity, thought Adrian,
suddenly. O.K., so he was going to be vain.

'Go back?'

'Yes.'

'But ... ' Adrian paused, aware of the artificiality.
'But why? What good will it do?'

'My family are being persecuted.'

'You don't know that.'

Pavel snorted a laugh. 'Don't be stupid,' he said. 'You
know it and I know it and everyone knows it. They're
tried, convicted and condemned.'

'But what good will your going back achieve?' queried
Adrian. He stopped, considering, thinking beyond the
need to justify himself at any later meetings with Ebbetts.
Whatever happened, he was to be fired. That was inevitable. But if he managed to keep Pavel as well as Bennovitch then he would have performed a service. The noun
rang in his mind, like church bells on Sunday. A service.
To what or to whom? To Britain. The pomposity jarred
him. It sounded like a line from one of the memoirs, one
of those 'why I did it' accounts from a politician anxious
to write his own history. 'I did it for my country.' It

didn't sound right without a trumpet fanfare. All right, Adrian decided, to Britain. But to himself as well. No one else would know, certainly. Miss Aimes would still despise him and so would Anita and Ebbetts and Sir William. And perhaps even Sir Jocelyn. But he wouldn't despise himself. He would have tried and it would be something to recall with ... yes, with pride and he was going to need some memory to support himself in the coming months.

'Viktor,' he began, slowly. 'Now let's think about this. When we began talking, four days ago, we established a code, an understanding if you like. I was honest with you and you respected it. And I'm being honest now, completely honest. You abandoned them. You discarded your wife and Georgi and young Valentina and you decided to come here. What good will you do by going back? It can't save them. Nothing can, not now. Going back would be an empty gesture.'

'I'll be with them.'

Adrian waited, preparing the moment. God, he thought, what a shit. His new word. His new self-description. Adrian Dodds, shit.

'Oh, for Christ's sake, Viktor,' — even the protest sounded false — 'what does that mean? What good will it do? If they're on trial, your going back won't stop the proceedings. It will just add another person in the dock.'

Pavel began another tour of the room. 'I'll be with them,' he insisted, doggedly. 'I'll die with them.'

Adrian's attitude hardened.

'Viktor, believe one thing. Believe and accept that you've lost whatever influence you had in the Soviet Union. The day — that day — when you walked away from the Paris show, you destroyed everything — your prestige, your importance, your ability to dictate terms. You're lost now. You're a traitor, a defector. To Russia, you're a "nothing" man. It's over, Viktor. Four weeks ago, you were the most important man in Russia. Today, you're nothing.'

'Except a target.'

The reply surprised Adrian. 'No one knows where you are. You're safe.'

He gave the cue to Pavel. 'But they're not. I want to go back. The embassy man said if I went back, everything would be as it was before I left.'

'Oh Viktor,' rebuked Adrian. 'You don't believe that and neither do I. If you go back, you're dead.'

'So are they.'

'So they are, whatever happens.'

'But I can die with them.'

'That's a stupid attitude.'

'I don't give a fuck for your opinion of my attitude.'

Pavel used the Russian expression and Adrian thought it sounded better than English.

'You can't stop me,' insisted Pavel. 'The embassy official said if I wanted to go back, there was no way you could prevent it.'

Adrian sighed. 'No Viktor, there isn't. We can't hold you against your will.'

He hesitated, then pressed on, brutally. 'They'll die,' he said. 'Valentina and Georgi and your wife. They will be tried and put into a labour camp and there they will die. It will happen whether or not you go back. Don't be so bloody stupid. There's only one way you can attack the Soviet Union for what they're going to do. That is by staying here, in the West.'

'If I go back, I'll be killed,' said Pavel, bluntly.

Adrian thought he was wavering.

'Probably. Or sent to Potma for twenty years.'

Adrian had wrongly assessed the Russian's remark.

'So I'll go back,' said Pavel, 'I'll go back and die, with my family.'

124

'Don't be so bloody stupid,' repeated Adrian, feeling he was losing the argument.

For a moment, Pavel looked at him. Then he said, 'Don't lecture me about love.'

I'm the last person to imagine I have the qualification, thought Adrian, I'm an accepted failure.

'I wasn't lecturing about love. I was arguing against the stupidity of it all.'

'Love isn't stupid,' said Pavel.

'No,' agreed Adrian, 'no, it isn't.'

'I'm going back,' insisted Pavel. 'I'm going back to die. I'm not going to tell you another thing. From this moment, our co-operation ends. I want to see the man from the embassy again.'

'You're stupid,' shouted Adrian.

Pavel remained silent.

'So everybody dies,' said Adrian, trying for a shock effect. 'It's so pointless.'

'Everything is pointless, without people you love and who love you,' retorted Pavel.

Adrian winced at the Russian's remark. A discussion about romance from a space scientist. He hadn't expected that.

'What does it prove, to die?' asked Adrian.

'Nothing,' admitted Pavel, immediately. 'But don't be obtuse. I'm not trying to prove anything, not to you, anyway. If my family die, I'll die with them. I'll have proved something to myself, that's all. I've a lot of people to make amends to.'

'There's no argument I can put up, is there,' said Adrian, resigned.

'No. None at all.'

For a long while, neither spoke. Then Adrian said, 'It's odd. I think we could have been friends.'

Pavel considered the remark. 'Yes,' he said, 'I think we might.'

'Others will try and persuade you to stay, after me,' warned Adrian.

'Tell them not to bother,' said Pavel. 'It won't do any good.'

'I'll try. But they might not take any notice.'

The Russian came back and sat opposite. 'Has this been a personal failure for you?' he asked, with sudden awareness.

'Yes,' admitted Adrian.

'I'm sorry.'

'It was hardly your fault.'

Suddenly Pavel extended his hand. Adrian sat for a moment, staring at the Russian. Then he took it and they shook hands.

'Goodbye,' said Pavel.

'There'll be other meetings,' said Adrian.

'But they'll be different from today's.'

'Yes,' agreed Adrian. 'They'll be different.'

'So — goodbye.'

'Goodbye.'

Chapter Eleven

Sir Jocelyn's secretary handed him the cup and he smiled appreciatively, enjoying the aroma of the Earl Grey. Sir Jocelyn is making amends, he decided.

'So you were right,' said the Permanent Secretary.

Adrian made a dismissive gesture and sipped his tea. 'But I don't know why or how I was right,' he said, modestly.

'Could it be that there isn't any other reason for his wanting to return, other than this fantastic feeling he has for his family?'

'Yes,' agreed Adrian, slowly. 'Yes, it could be. If you can accept that for four or five days, through some mental aberration, he relegated that love to be the last rather than the first consideration.'

Binns smiled. 'Here we go again,' he said. 'Around and around on the roundabout without knowing where to get off.'

'I wonder if we'll ever know,' mused Adrian.

'He hasn't tried to influence Bennovitch in any way, has he?' asked Binns, suddenly. 'I mean, there hasn't been anything that has not been made clear on the tapes, any pressure for the other man to return to Russia as well?'

Adrian shook his head.

'No,' he said, 'nothing at all. There has never been a moment when they've been alone together. I've been with them all the time. Naturally they've discussed the family: after all, Valentina is Bennovitch's sister. But from what Pavel said about the purge that followed Bennovitch's defection, it would be a deterrent rather than an encouragement to return.'

'I don't suppose ... ' Binns began and then stopped, shaking his head at a ridiculous thought.

'What?'

'No, nothing. It's too stupid to consider.'

'The whole thing is stupid,' prompted Adrian.

'I just wondered if Pavel had come to do any harm to his former partner.'

'Physical harm?' queried Adrian, and when Binns nodded, said immediately, 'Oh no, that's impossible too. Nothing has passed between them, like any drug or anything like that, because they've both been searched before and after each meeting. That would have uncovered any weapon, too. And what would it have gained? Physical violence would have given us a reason for holding Pavel indefinitely and keeping him away from his family. But the idea of Pavel harming Bennovitch is unthinkable for one main reason — apart from his family, I would think there is no one Pavel loves more than Bennovitch. Their feeling for each other is almost unnatural.'

And I should know about unnatural feelings, he thought. I'd probably be considered an expert.

Binns sighed, shaking his head. 'I told you it was stupid,' he said.

The Permanent Secretary toyed with a paper-knife for several moments. Then he said, 'You know Pavel has asked to see you again?'

Adrian nodded. The meeting at which Pavel had said he wanted to return to Russia had been three days before and immediately Ebbetts had learned of the request, he had suspended Adrian from the debriefing of the older Russian.

'How have the other meetings gone?' asked Adrian.

Binns smiled. 'Disastrously,' he said. 'The Prime Minister has tried everything. He sent down two separate men to take up where you'd left off and then when they failed, he allowed two men from the American embassy to go down.'

'He let the Americans go in?' asked Adrian, surprised.

'He was desperate,' said Binns. 'And so were they. I've never heard so many offers made in a shorter period. If Pavel had accepted, only the President would have been more important than he was.'

Adrian smiled at the sarcasm. 'But he didn't accept?'

'Of course not,' said Binns. 'He treated them all with complete contempt. He'd been well briefed by his own embassy man. He merely parried all the questions, as if he were playing with them almost, and then repeated his request for consular access to his embassy, telling us it was illegal to hold him. The only positive thing he's said is to ask for another meeting with you. He refers to you as the only intelligent Englishman he's met since he came here.'

Adrian grimaced at the flattery. 'How does the Prime Minister react to *that* when he hears it on tape?'

'With whitefaced silence,' replied Binns. 'I would have thought he owes you an apology.'

'But I doubt that I'm going to get it.'

'So do I,' said Binns. 'He wants to see you too.'

Adrian was surprised. 'What for?'

'I don't know. It's been arranged for Pavel to be handed over to the Russians this afternoon. I thought you could see him, travel part of the way back to London with him and then we'd go over to Downing Street at about four. That's the time the P.M. has suggested.'

Adrian remained frowning. 'Is there any chance of a change of mind about my staying in the department?'

The question seemed to embarrass the Permanent Secretary. 'I don't know,' he said. 'Nobody has said anything.'

Adrian leaned back comfortably in his chair.

'Do you know what I think?' he said.

'What?'

'I think that the Prime Minister, who might owe me an apology, has an altogether different role selected for me. Somebody has got to be blamed for this. And I think I'm going to be the one.'

Binns shifted uncomfortably in his chair.

'I think so, too,' he said.

Pavel was waiting for him in the room where they had had all their meetings, like a tourist expecting a holiday coach, his raincoat over the chair, a small cardboard suitcase at his feet.

He saw Adrian look at the case.

'I did have a leather one,' said the Russian, proudly. 'It was very good. I'd had it for a long time. But I had to leave it behind in Paris.'

Adrian nodded. 'Of course,' he said.

'I could only bring the photograph,' Pavel went on. He reached into his raincoat and pulled out the silver frame and opened it.

'Soon,' he said, as if he were making himself a promise. 'Very soon now.'

He looked back to Adrian.

'I've seen a lot of people since our last meeting.'

'Really?'

'There were two Englishmen and then some Americans. All the Americans could talk about was how much money I could earn in the United States. They said they would award me three hundred thousand dollars a year. Is that a high salary for the United States?'

'Very,' said Adrian. Christ, he thought, they weren't just desperate. They were frantic.

'And they also said I could have some stock options in a company. What is that?'

Adrian smiled. 'It's like owning part of a company,' he said. 'Everyone has a share and you get paid a dividend on your share holdings.'

'Owning part of the company?' queried Pavel. 'Like communism?'

Adrian laughed outright. 'Not quite,' he said. He wondered if they were still recording the conversations. He hoped so.

'Were you surprised I wanted to see you?'

'A little.'

'I was worried.'

'About what?'

'Alexandre. Have you seen him?'

Adrian nodded.

'How has he taken it?'

'Badly.'

Adrian confined himself to an easy answer. Badly: that's putting it mildly, he thought. Bennovitch had retreated completely, barely communicating with the security men guarding him, refusing food, almost having to be forced to wash and shave himself.

The tiny Russian was bowed under an enormous guilt complex, made aware by Pavel's decision to return that the persecution of those still in Russia and of the older scientist stemmed from his initial defection. It was a burden that Adrian doubted Bennovitch was mentally able to support. The breakdown wasn't months away now. It couldn't be more than a few weeks.

'Alexandre is not well,' said Pavel, suddenly.

'Not well?'

The Russian tapped his head. 'His work is a strain,' he said, expressing himself badly. 'He has a brilliant mind, but he can't accept it. He seems to think that he should not possess the gifts he has and so, for no reason, he feels guilty. He will produce some outstanding work and then apologize when he's presenting it. Do you know,

sometimes I suspect he purposely made mistakes in calculations, knowing I would spot them, so that he would
be shown to be fallible.'

So the depression was registering, even in Russia,
thought Adrian. He wondered if anybody else had noticed
it from the transcription of the tapes.

'I have a favour to ask,' said Pavel.

'What?'

'I have written Alexandre a letter. Would you see that
he gets it?'

Adrian hesitated. 'I will have to read it,' he said,
doubtfully. 'And then, the decision will not be wholly
mine.'

'Of course.'

The Russian held out the unsealed envelope and Adrian
took it.

'I'd like to read it now,' said Adrian.

'Please.'

It was a short note, without any introduction, barely
covering half a sheet of paper:

Forgive me for what I have done. But my family
mean more to me than life itself. I shall care for
Valentina. I promise you that. Goodbye, dear
Friend.

'Will he be allowed to have it?' asked Pavel.

Adrian looked up. 'I don't see why not.'

'Today?'

'That might not be possible,' replied Adrian, cau-
tiously.

'As soon as you can?'

'I promise.'

'Thank you.'

A security man entered and Pavel got up eagerly. He
seemed surprised when Adrian got into the car with him.

'You're not coming to the embassy?' he said.

'No. I'm just travelling part of the way.'

The enclosed vehicle edged out into the traffic and began the northward journey. Pavel sat quite relaxed, the case between his legs, the raincoat across his lap. He kept looking at his watch, as if eager for the journey to be completed.

Going home to die, thought Adrian. Going home to die and he was impatient about it. Still the uncertainty nagged at Adrian's mind.

'Viktor,' he said, abruptly.

The Russian looked at him.

'Do you know, I doubted you from the very beginning.'

Pavel just stared.

'I never believed you had any intention of permanently defecting,' continued Adrian. 'I said so, in my first report.'

'Were you believed?' asked Pavel, guardedly.

'No,' Adrian shook his head. 'No. I was overruled.'

'And now you're vindicated?'

'I wish it were as simple as that,' said Adrian, smiling. 'No, I've not been vindicated.'

Pavel frowned. 'I don't understand.'

'I'm not sure that I do, completely,' said the Englishman. They drove for several miles without speaking. Then Adrian said, 'Was it genuine, Viktor? Did you intend to defect?'

Pavel took a long time to answer and when he did so, he looked directly at Adrian.

'Believe me,' he said, 'if I could get my family out of the Soviet Union, I would choose to work here.'

'That wasn't the question.'

'But that is my answer.'

The car slowed and Adrian saw they had reached the spot where he was to leave.

'I'm getting out here,' he said.

'You'll see Alexandre gets the letter?'

'I'll do my utmost.'

'It's important.'

Adrian nodded. He hesitated, half out of the car, then turned back, aware of the impatience of the security cars in front and behind.

'I'm right, aren't I, Viktor? You never intended to stay?'

The Russian stared at him, expressionless.

'Goodbye,' he said.

'Goodbye,' said Adrian.

He stood in the side-road that had been selected as a safe disembarkation point. There were motorcycle policemen at either end and he would be overlooked from several windows, he knew. The Rover pulled away, rejoined the traffic stream and disappeared from view after a few moments. I'll never know, thought Adrian. Now, I'll never know.

Chapter Twelve

They sat in the small room again, off the Cabinet chamber, and met as before, Ebbetts and the Foreign Secretary on one side of the table, Binns and Adrian on the other.

Between them lay the transcripts of every conversation that had been held with the two defectors, an unnecessary reminder of failure. But this time there was an anonymous secretary sitting at the far end of the table, notebook and pen before him.

History will have its records, thought Adrian. When the archives are opened in thirty years' time the blunder of failing to keep two of the most important defectors ever to leave Russia working together as a team would be shown to be that of Adrian Dodds, thirty-five, a senior debriefing officer at the Home Office.

He wondered if that were the sole reason for this afternoon's summons, the need to get the blame established for later reference. Was he getting too cynical? Perhaps. Then again, perhaps not.

Ebbetts sat hunched in his chair, tapping the papers before him with a thin gold pencil, like a conductor trying to get a choir to sing in tune. His tune, thought Adrian. Ebbetts would have to be the composer, ensuring everyone got the words right.

The Foreign Secretary kept darting glances sideways, awaiting cues. Adrian suddenly thought how much better Sir William would be as premier than Ebbetts.

Ebbetts began speaking slowly, almost as if he were mouthing carefully rehearsed lines.

'In all my years as a politician,' he said, 'including those as Foreign Secretary when we previously held office, I do not think I have ever encountered a worse example of ineffectual, stupid blundering than it's been my misfortune to witness over the last two weeks. I've made this clear at the previous meeting, Dodds, and I'm going to say it again, just to get the record straight ... '

He paused, glancing sideways almost imperceptibly at the secretary. ' ... that I hold you completely and utterly responsible for the failure to get Pavel to stay in this country.'

' ... utterly responsible ... ' echoed Fornham.

Ebbetts extended his hand, palm upwards, theatrically. 'We held in our hands the greatest opportunity for a decade, perhaps longer. If we could have successfully debriefed Pavel and Bennovitch together, there is nothing we could not have known about the space plans of the Warsaw Pact countries for years to come.'

He slapped the extended hand down on the papers.

'It's all been thrown away,' he said.

' ... thrown away,' intoned the Foreign Secretary.

Adrian was breathing evenly, feeling quite composed. He was surprised that there was no nervousness. Seven, maybe eight days ago there would have been. His hands would have been wet with anxiety and the words would have jumbled incoherently in his mind, like leaves in a wind. But not any more. He didn't need a lavatory, either. If Ebbetts wanted the record straight, then let it be.

'When we met in this room, a few days ago,' he started out, 'I warned you that I did not think Pavel's defection was genuine ... '

' ... a stupid impression,' Sir William cut in.

' ... a stupid impression that proved to be one hundred per cent accurate. As we are getting records straight, let another thing be noted. I said then that there was an ulterior motive in Viktor Pavel's defection and I repeat it again ... '

'What ulterior motive?'

Ebbetts, the practised politician, saw the weak spot and struck at it.

Adrian swallowed. 'I don't know,' he said, ignoring Ebbetts's expression of disgust. 'But I would have known. I would have known if I had been allowed to conduct the debriefing properly and under my own terms of reference instead of being forced to rush the two men together, grab what we could from them and then offer them like bait to America, all for political expediency.'

'That's impertinence,' snapped Ebbetts, looking again at the secretary.

'Dodds, really ... ' began Sir Jocelyn, from his right.

'Impertinent, maybe,' admitted Adrian. 'But true. Completely and utterly true. Pavel wasn't a stupid man. He was, I think, one of the most intelligent men I have ever met. It was ridiculous, laughable even, to expect that we could get anything from him in two or three days, like a country policeman questioning a child stealing apples. I should have had a month with the man, at least, a month with just the two of us together, before we even considered linking him with Bennovitch.'

He paused, breathless. He was destroying a career and enjoying every moment of it.

'You said a few moments ago that we had missed the opportunity of a decade in losing Pavel. I'll extend that. We've lost the opportunity of a lifetime. I saw him work, albeit briefly, with Bennovitch and it was staggering. Their worth to the West would have been incalculable. But I completely refuse to accept any responsibility or blame for losing that opportunity. You ordered the debriefing to be speeded up and you stipulated the manner in which it would be done. I merely followed those in-structions — under protest.'

When the meeting had begun Ebbetts had been pale, white-faced almost, and completely under control. Now he was flushed with anger and Adrian noticed that his earlobes were bright red, as if he were wearing earrings. He was suddenly seized with the desire to laugh and immediately recognized the tip of hysteria. Consciously he controlled it. Don't let me break down now, he thought, there'll never be another moment like this and I don't want it dismissed as the outburst that precluded a nervous breakdown.

Another thought came, completely sobering him. If he collapsed, then Ebbetts would have a reason for destroying the record of the meeting.

'Have you forgotten who I am?' began Ebbetts, pompously.

'No, sir, I have not. Neither have I lost sight of the fact that I have been impertinent and also disrespectful to your office. For that, I apologize.'

'But not to me?'

Adrian hesitated. The opportunity was there and if he took it, he could retreat. For what? I've finished running, he decided. He stayed silent.

'I see,' said Ebbetts, stiffly. The colour was leaving his face now. He spread his hands, another practised move, and said, 'All right. Then let's examine the facts.'

Suddenly Adrian felt scared. He was more intelligent than Ebbetts, he was sure of that. But he did not think he was cleverer. Neither did he think he could match him in debate, certainly not a debate that would centre around a weakness in his argument, the ulterior reason for which Pavel had defected. In a point by point examination of the facts, Ebbetts would win.

'I will concede,' started the Prime Minister, 'that your hunch about his deciding to go back to his own country has proved correct. The point I have been making and which I feel is brought out in these transcripts' — he

138

patted the papers in front of him — 'is that because of your lamentable handling of the man, the idea of returning was allowed to build up in his mind. Look at the first interview. Your confirming his fears about his family, rather than trying to subdue them … '

Adrian sighed. 'How many more times do we have to go over this? There was a point in doing that, a point which I think is also shown in the transcript. I have already said Pavel was an intelligent man. The only way to conduct a debriefing of a man of that intellect is to gain his respect and the only way to do that is to be honest with him. He *knew* what would happen to his family if he stayed here. His questions to me were little more than rhetorical. For me to have dismissed them as unfounded would have destroyed any hope of establishing a relationship.'

Ebbetts nodded. 'But that's no explanation for your arrogance,' he said, definitely. 'You set out, consciously, to dismiss Pavel's importance in his own eyes, importance you now admit is unrivalled in the West … '

'But I didn't,' protested Adrian, exasperated, 'I've explained that, too. I had to dominate the examination. If I'd let Pavel lead, it could have taken months to reach the limited points we got to in less than a week. He was so over-confident … '

'Over-confident!' sneered Ebbetts. 'Crying at your second meeting … refusing to go out for exercise until it was dark. Is that your idea of over-confidence?'

Suddenly Adrian laughed. It was an odd, disjointed sound that jarred in the quietness of the room.

Ebbetts stared at him, the beginning of a smile on his face, imagining the hysteria that had frightened Adrian earlier.

'Dodds?' he said, doubtfully, 'are you all right?'

The question was perfectly pitched, showing just the right degree of solicitude.

Adrian laughed again, the sound controlled now, shaking his head.

'Oh my God,' he said. 'How brilliant. How incredibly, utterly brilliant.'

The three men looked blankly at him. Even the secretary, sitting at the end of the table, had stopped writing and was staring.

'I know it,' he said, softly. 'The reason. I know the reason. It was obvious all along, and we missed it.'

He straightened, looking straight at the Premier.

'We've just witnessed the most incredible attempt ever made by the Soviet Union to liquidate a defector,' he announced.

Ebbetts was serious now, head cocked, alert.

'What the hell are you talking about?'

'How could the Russians get to Bennovitch?' asked Adrian. 'How could they possibly get to the man, discover what he'd told us and liquidate him? There was no way, no way at all. Except by offering a bigger bait and we took it, like amateurs, like stumbling, idiotic amateurs. For the past week all we've thought about was Pavel and Pavel never intended to stay here. They *knew* we'd put them together ... '

He paused, allowing himself the sarcasm. 'Perhaps not as quickly as we did, but they knew we would link them. And we sat and let them talk and I thought they were working out some new problem that had arisen and all Pavel was doing was determining to what degree we'd progressed with Bennovitch's debriefing ... '

He thought back to Pavel's remark in the car taking them to London for the meeting with the embassy official, the clue that had been given him and which he'd ignored —'they just glitter there, the winning posts for a race of giants.'

'You pinpointed it,' he said to Ebbetts. 'You said it and even now you don't realize it. The stars. It's the stars.'

140

The room was completely silent. Everyone sat motionless.

'Pavel didn't go out only at night because he was scared. He went out at night because only then was there any point in his doing so.'

Ebbetts shook his head.

'You're not making sense … '

'Stars,' shouted Adrian. 'That's what he wanted to see, stars. What was Pavel before he entered space science? What did he read at university? It was all there for us to see, in his history, but we missed it. He studied navigation, with the emphasis on stellar navigation. Pavel knew just where he was in England within minutes of walking out into the garden at Pulborough on the first night, just by looking upwards. And he knows where Bennovitch is being held, by the same method. It was dark when we left Petworth after the meeting and we paused by the car and I thought he was just getting a breath of air. But he wasn't. He was checking the star reference again. Put against the timed distance it took to drive back from one house to the other, which he simply had to time by checking his wrist watch and the aerial description of the house which he got from the helicopter, which they'll compare with satellite shots of southern England, the Russians will by now know exactly where Bennovitch is being held. He's got the aerial picture and the triangular fix, London, Pulborough and Petworth.'

He stopped, unable to understand why the others in the room were not as excited as he was.

'That was Pavel's reason for defecting … the job he was sent here to do. He was marking Bennovitch out as a target.'

Ebbetts cupped his hands across his stomach, complacently.

'I've never heard anything so ridiculous in my life,' he said.

' ... ridiculous ... ' agreed Fornham.

'I'm right,' insisted Adrian.

Ebbetts shrugged. 'Whether you are or not doesn't matter a damn,' he said. 'I'm well aware how low you regard our intelligence here, Dodds, but we're not all fools. It occurred to me, even before your far-fetched theories, that there was a security risk involving Benno-vitch. I wanted to salvage something out of the mess, so I gave instructions that he was to be moved, this afternoon.'

'No,' shouted Adrian, half rising from his seat. 'For God's sake, don't move him. That's just what they'd expect ... what they'd want even. Inside the house he's safe. They can't get to him there because he's too well guarded. But outside he becomes just the target they want.'

Ebbetts waved his hand impatiently, like someone flicking away an irritating insect.

'This meeting is over, Dodds. There's nothing to be gained by continuing the discussion and I would strongly recommend your seeing a doctor ... '

He stopped, disturbed by the door opening behind the note-taker. Adrian recognized the Prime Minister's principal private secretary.

The man walked up to the Premier, bent and whispered to him for several moments. Halfway through Ebbetts turned, staring at Adrian. The colour flooded back into his face and the earrings returned.

The P.P.S. stood back but didn't leave the room. At the bottom of the table, the other secretary shuffled the pages of his notebook and the rustling sound seemed loud in the room.

Ebbetts coughed, looking down at the table, as if preparing himself. Then he said, 'Alexandre Bennovitch was being moved at about five o'clock this afternoon. We were taking him into Kent. The car in which he was travelling and the back-up vehicle were ambushed within two hundred yards of leaving the Petworth mansion. By the time the lead car stopped and the security men got back, the gunmen had gone ... '

He hesitated, as if details were important. 'They used Uzzi machine-guns. We've had a ballistics report. I suppose they thought Israeli weapons would create some sort of international problem and Kaleshnikovs would be too obvious.'

There was another pause. Then he said, speaking directly to Adrian, 'Bennovitch is dead. So are the guards in the two cars.'

Adrian felt no surprise. It was just the expected con-firmation. Poor Alexandre, he thought, poor little fat, mentally disturbed Alexandre. So everybody had lost. He and Ebbetts and Bennovitch and Pavel. And Britain and Russia and America. Everyone a loser.

He touched his pocket, feeling the letter which Pavel had asked him to deliver. He died without knowing the man he regarded as a father was sorry, thought Adrian. He wondered if there had been a moment, just before death, when Bennovitch had realized what had happened.

Ebbetts stood up, suddenly, and walked from the room, leaving the Foreign Secretary sitting there.

'Good Lord,' said the aristocrat.

Bad show, thought Adrian. At this moment, he's thinking, what a bad show.

'Bad show,' confirmed Sir William Fornham, initiating the first sentence Adrian could recall.

Chapter Thirteen

They had almost completed the journey back from Downing Street before Binns spoke.

'Well,' he said. 'You were right.'

Adrian didn't respond.

'How does it feel?'

Adrian considered the question. 'There isn't a feeling,' he said. Then he conceded, 'I suppose it vindicates the department.'

'Yes,' agreed Binns, as if it had occurred to him for the first time. 'I suppose it does.'

'I don't imagine it'll change anything as far as I'm concerned,' said Adrian.

They showed their security passes at the door and moved into the lift.

'I don't know,' said Binns. 'He hates being wrong, publicly wrong, and he's certainly shown to be that. But it could rebound in your favour. He can hardly dismiss someone who was so accurate, can he?'

Adrian shrugged, not bothering to reply.

'Doesn't it matter any more?' asked Binns.

'I don't know,' replied Adrian, 'I really don't know.'

They got out of the lift and began walking down the echoing corridor.

'I suppose we can completely stop any publicity about the assassination?' said Adrian.

Binns nodded. 'Quite easily. I checked before we left Downing Street. Apparently the cars had hardly left the house and our own people were the first on the scene. We'll handle the whole thing.'

'I'm surprised they were able to get away quite so easily.'

'It was very professional,' admitted Binns, 'but very simple. They knew all they had to do was regain the main road. We're hardly going to have a running gun-battle on the A3 with a car bearing C.D. plates, are we?'

They got to the door of Binns's office and stopped.

'Tomorrow,' said Binns. 'Come and see me tomorrow and we'll sort it out.'

He hesitated. Then he added, 'That's if you want to.'

Adrian smiled. 'I'll tell you tomorrow,' he said. 'At the moment, I'm not sure.'

'And Adrian.'

'What?'

'Well done. And I'm sorry for my doubt.'

Adrian nodded and walked on down the corridor to his own office. He's stopped stuttering again, Adrian thought. I've recovered a friend.

Miss Aimes was burrowing into the drawers of her desk when he entered and Adrian paused just inside the door, surprised at her activity.

'Oh,' she said, 'you're back.'

As always, there was a mixture of surprise and disappointment in the greeting. Adrian stared hopefully. Bending might have displaced the wig. She patted it, needlessly. As always, it was corrugated in perfect order and he sighed, resigned to never knowing.

'The meeting finished early,' he explained. Why was it she always prompted explanations?

'Guess what has happened?' demanded the woman.

'I'm sorry?'

'You'll never guess what's happened. He's come back.'

'Who has?'

'The pigeon. The pigeon with the broken beak. It was on the window-sill this morning when I came in.'

Adrian turned to the window. The bird stiff-legged its

way up and down on jealous patrol, chest puffed with pride of ownership. Its injury gave it a lopsided grin and Adrian grinned back at it.

All my friends are coming back, he decided.

'I gave it some biscuit crumbs,' reported Miss Aimes, appearing anxious to prove her initiative. 'It seemed hungry.'

'Thank you,' said Adrian. He would have to buy another packet of biscuits. But plain, not chocolate. He hoped his successor, if there were to be one, would take over the guardianship. Perhaps he would if before he went he got in a reasonable supply of food, maybe some bird-seed even.

He sat at his desk, cupping his head in his hands, suddenly tired. It was all over. There was nothing left to do, apart from a few tidying-up reports. There *was* a feeling, he decided, thinking back to Binns's question. It was an emptiness, just a hollow emptiness. And if that's all it was, it was hardly worth all the effort.

He realized he hadn't bothered to protect his trousers with his seat pad. So what? Perhaps he wouldn't need it any more, after tomorrow. He wondered whether to make a present of it to Miss Aimes.

'Can I have a word with you?'

Adrian looked up, frowning. If he hadn't known his secretary better he would have imagined a note of servility in her voice.

'Of course. What is it?'

She paused, as if she had difficulty in selecting her words.

'I'm leaving,' she said, bluntly.

'What?'

'I'm leaving. I've put in for a transfer and it's been granted. It'll mean going on to a higher grade.'

'Oh,' he said. She would expect more. He groped for the necessary pleasantries.

'I'm sorry,' he said, untruthfully.

'So am I,' she replied, untruthfully.

This is ridiculous, he thought.

'Where are you going?'

She smirked, glad he'd asked.

'Sir Jocelyn's secretary is leaving. She's pregnant, you know.'

'No,' replied Adrian. 'I didn't know.'

Oh God, he thought, Miss Aimes and Earl Grey tea. Poor Sir Jocelyn.

'I'll miss you,' he said, feeling the remark was necessary.

'I regret leaving,' she said, joining in the charade. 'But I didn't think I could miss the opportunity. It means another £300 a year.'

'Oh, of course not,' agreed Adrian, quickly, 'I quite understand.'

They sat staring at each other, completely out of words. There should be instructions, thought Adrian, a book on how to say goodbye to a secretary you didn't mind losing.

'When are you leaving?' he asked.

'Next Friday.'

'Oh well, there's another week then.'

He wondered why he'd said that. It didn't mean anything. He'd have to buy her a farewell gift, he supposed, some perfume or some flowers or something. He smiled, amused at a sudden thought. Or a home perm.

Miss Aimes smiled back at him. 'Yes,' she said, 'there's another week.'

'Would you mind if I left early tonight?' she said, predictably. She saw the look on his face and added, 'I'm going up to see Sir Jocelyn's secretary, to learn the routine.'

'Oh no,' he said. 'No, of course not. I'll see you tomorrow.'

'You're coming straight here?' she asked, perturbed at the thought of having to arrive reasonably near time.

'Yes.' he said. 'Straight here.'

'Oh.' Disappointment again.

'Good night.'

'Good night.'

Adrian stood at the window after Miss Aimes had gone, looking out at the bird. A pigeon with a broken beak in exchange for Miss Aimes, he thought. One bird for another. Comparably, the pigeon walked more elegantly. He smiled, happy at the swop.

He felt in his pocket, where Pavel's letter was. Against it was another, one that had been delivered that morning. He didn't feel like it, but it had to be done. It took him thirty minutes to reach the flat where Anita was living with the other woman. He nodded to the porter as he walked in and the man returned the greeting, recognizing him. The medal ribbon had been sewn on the correct way, Adrian noticed.

'They expecting you?'

'No.'

'I'd better check then.'

'Yes. You'd better.'

The porter mumbled into the house phone and then said, 'Miss Sinclair says to go up.'

She was waiting for him by the open door when he stepped out of the lift, smiling pleasantly. Adrian thought how beautiful she was.

'Hello.'

'Hello.'

They shook hands. Again he was surprised by how soft and feminine her grip was.

'Whisky, brandy or sherry?' she asked, closing the door.

Just like the housemaster's wife, he decided again.

'Whisky.'

She handed him the drink, took her usual brandy and sat opposite.

'How are you?' she asked, as if they were old friends.

148

He shrugged, undecided. 'All right,' he said.

'You don't sound very sure.'

'I'm not.'

'Oh.' She sat, waiting.

'I had a letter from my solicitor this morning,' he said. 'He's been told by Anita's solicitor that there was some difficulty in getting any instructions from her. Apparently she isn't replying to their letters.'

'No,' agreed Anne. 'She isn't.'

She nodded to the hall table and Adrian twisted, seeing the buff envelopes.

He turned back to her. 'I don't understand.'

'Anita isn't here any more,' she said.

'Not here?'

'She walked out, several days ago.'

'You mean ... that you and she ... ?'

'I mean that we had a blazing row and she packed her bags and cleared out and we're not living together any more.'

'Oh ... ' said Adrian. 'I'm ... ' he managed to stop before completing the sentence, but Anne smiled, guessing he was going to say he was sorry.

'You're a funny man, Adrian.'

He said nothing.

'I don't know where she is,' she continued, anticipating his question. 'I thought she might even have gone back to you, but obviously, she hasn't.'

'No,' he said, 'she hasn't.'

'Is there anywhere else she could have gone?'

Adrian thought, trying to remember relatives.

'No,' he said, 'I don't think there is.'

'Would you take her back?'

He jerked up at her question. 'What?'

'She believes that you'd take her back if she asked you. She's probably trying to pluck up courage. Would you?'

Again Adrian hesitated before replying. 'No,' he said,

after several moments. 'No, I don't think I would. Not now.'

'I'm surprised,' said Anne Sinclair.

Adrian smiled at her. 'To be perfectly honest, so am I,' he said. He added, seriously, 'But I don't think I would.'

'Poor Anita,' said the woman.

'Do you think she'll contact you again?' asked Adrian.

Anne laughed. 'No,' she said. 'No, I don't. She quit work as well. Nobody knows where she is.'

'If she does get in touch, will you ask her to call me?'

'Of course.'

Anne was silent for a while, and then she said, 'I think you *would* take her back, Adrian. I don't think you'd want to, but I think you would. You're too nice. You couldn't turn her away if you wanted to.'

'Could you?' he said.

'Yes,' said the woman. 'Yes, I could say "no". But then, I'm *not* so nice as you are.'

There was a sudden sound from the doorway and then footsteps and Adrian turned. A slim girl stood in the entrance, her red hair tied in a pony-tail and with hardly any makeup. She was very slim, boyish almost, dressed in tight fitting jeans and a shaggy lambskin waistcoat. A disillusioned hippie, judged Adrian. A new week, a new experience. She blushed, deeply embarrassed, at finding someone other than Anne Sinclair in the room.

'Hello darling,' greeted Anne. 'This is Adrian, Adrian Dodds.'

Adrian stood up and turned to face her.

'Hello,' he said.

'Hello,' replied the girl, still confused. She looked at the older woman for guidance, got none and then came back to Adrian. There was a long silence and Adrian got the impression that Anne was enjoying it.

'I'll ... ah ... I'll make some coffee. Would you like

some coffee?' asked the young girl, ignoring the whisky glass in his hand.

Adrian smiled at her, feeling great pity.

'Yes. Yes please, I would,' he said.

They stood watching as the girl, still wearing her lambskin coat, escaped into the kitchen.

Adrian turned back to Anne, who shrugged.

'Life must go on,' she said.

'Yes,' said Adrian, 'yes, of course.' He paused. 'I think I'll go before she comes back.'

She looked towards the kitchen. 'Yes,' she said, 'that would be kind.'

She held out her hand. 'Goodbye,' she said. 'We won't meet again, will we?'

'No,' said Adrian. 'We won't.'

'You know,' said Anne Sinclair, at the doorway, 'I wish I were as kind as you.'

There was a mirror in the lift and Adrian stared at his reflection as he descended. I haven't thought about it for a long time, he thought. All this trouble and suicide hasn't occurred to me. He suddenly felt very happy.

The lift stopped and the doors opened, but Adrian make no attempt to leave. He stood, studying his reflection, like someone introduced to a stranger. He was aware of the porter staring at him, curiously, but he didn't care. The buzzer sounded as someone summoned the lift several floors above.

'You all right?' called the porter.

Reluctantly Adrian got out. He smiled at the attendant.

'Yes,' he said, 'as a matter of fact I'm fine, just fine.'

He stopped. The porter wore a wig, an obvious National Health wig. He hadn't noticed that, either.

'Fine,' he repeated, 'just fine.'

The porter watched him walk out of the door.

'Bloody fool,' said the man, to himself.

Chapter Fourteen

Pavel sat alone in the reserved section of the Ilyushin airliner, watching as the plane taxied towards Sheremetyevo control tower, with its surround of coloured lights. In Paris once, many years before, he had been driven past a funfair and there had been several sideshows and amusement rides decorated the same way and he was always reminded of it when he arrived at Moscow airport. He had always regretted not stopping at that funfair, even riding like a child on one of the imitation animals constantly chasing its own tail.

This would be the last time, he realized suddenly. He would never again depart or arrive and be reminded of a Paris funfair he should have visited. He had made his last trip abroad, ever. He sighed and stood up, pulling his raincoat and cardboard case from the rack. It didn't matter. Only one thing mattered.

Everyone else was held while he disembarked, walking alone down the steps that had been run especially into the front of the aircraft.

There were a few militiamen around the car and Pavel saw he was to get a motorcycle escort into the capital. Everything is back to normal, he thought. A driver respectfully held the door open for him. Back in his accustomed environment, Pavel nodded curtly and handed his luggage to the man, then got into the gleaming black Zil without speaking. He stopped, half in, half out, still crouched.

Kaganov lounged in the back, in the far corner.

'Welcome back,' said the chairman.

Pavel completed his entry, wedging himself into the opposite corner. He did not return the greeting.

The driver turned, looking to Kaganov rather than Pavel for guidance. The chairman, who was wearing military uniform unmarked by any insignia, nodded and the car pulled out and a convoy formed around it.

'Welcome back,' repeated Kaganov. 'And my congratulations. You were very accurate. Everything went as planned.'

'You hardly thought I'd fail, did you?' snapped Pavel. He wore arrogance like an overcoat, a protection against the cold.

'No,' agreed Kaganov, pleasantly. 'We didn't think you'd fail.'

'What about my family?' asked Pavel.

'They're perfectly all right,' assured Kaganov. 'Just as we promised you they would be.'

'And Georgi?'

'He was brought back from the Chinese front two days ago. He's attached to the Kremlin now. He'll be home with you every weekend until he finishes his service.'

'I have your word?'

'I told you before you went,' rebuked Kaganov, mildly. 'If you kept your side of the bargain, we'd keep ours. Your family are in perfect health and looking forward to your return.'

The car was in the city now. They went by Krasnaya Ploshtchad and Pavel looked at the Kremlin beyond. It's beautiful, he thought. Beautiful and peaceful. Only people are ugly. They crossed Kammeni Bridge and turned right. Pavel looked into the park, where the trees were weeping their leaves at the thought of winter. A little month and it will be autumn, he thought. Everything will be dead, just like Bennovitch back there, all alone, in England.

'I'm interested in the person who debriefed you.'

Kaganov broke into the reverie and Pavel turned to him.

'What?'

'The man who debriefed you.' He made the pretence of taking a notebook from his greatcoat pocket and checking the name. 'Dodds, Adrian Dodds. According to what our people can gather at the embassy, the English regard him rather highly.'

Pavel remained looking across the car, saying nothing.

Kaganov reached into his briefcase at his feet and pulled out six photographs. Three were blurred, but the remainder were of good quality, although they had all obviously been taken by hidden cameras.

'What do you want me to do?'

'Identify him, if he's any of the men pictured here,' said Kaganov.

'What for?' asked Pavel, aware of the answer.

Kaganov laughed and Pavel saw his false teeth were made of steel, dull and grey looking. They made laughter a horrifying grimace. Many Russians had had them made like that during the war, Pavel remembered, but only a few had kept them, for affectation. It gave Pavel another reason for despising the man.

'Well,' said the chairman. 'It occurred to me that there might be some other misguided fools in the future who might think like your brother-in-law ... people who might find in Dodds just the sort of sympathy and understanding to unburden themselves ... '

He laughed again.

' ... So I thought we might safeguard ourselves by arranging an accident for Comrade Dodds, if we could discover what he looks like ... '

He splayed the photographs out, like a poker player revealing a winning hand. Adrian stared at Pavel from the second picture, one of the better ones. He was shown

154

getting out of a taxi, looking smarter than Pavel remembered him, wearing a suit that was crisp and well-pressed and with well-polished shoes.

'Take your time,' coaxed Kaganov. 'There's no hurry. Some of them aren't very good quality, but you'll understand that they weren't exactly taken under ideal circumstances.'

Dutifully Pavel went from print to print, then completed another survey, remaining expressionless. Then he looked up at Kaganov.

'He's not one of these men,' he said.

The other man frowned. 'Are you sure?' he said, quizzically.

'Are you doubting me?' the scientist demanded, refusing to be intimidated. 'I was with the man constantly for over a week. Is it likely I wouldn't be able to recognize him?'

'But the embassy were sure ... '

'Then the embassy are wrong,' snapped Pavel. 'And how can they be sure if they have to send six different pictures?'

Kaganov accepted the rebuke. Slowly he stored the photographs back into his case.

'Pity,' he said, mildly.

'Hardly a great loss,' said Pavel.

The chairman looked at him, curiously.

'The English might regard Dodds highly, but I thought he was a fool.'

'Really.' Doubt still tinged Kaganov's reactions.

'He accepted my defection completely, never doubting me for one moment,' lied Pavel. 'He can speak perfect Russian, certainly, but he's very naive. He's little more than a clerk, reciting questions that the experts have set, with little awareness of what they mean. Deviate from the list and he's completely lost.'

'Not worth killing, you mean?' said Kaganov.

Pavel stared at him. 'You are the man who decides who should live and die,' he said, 'not me. But I think you've overestimated Dodds.'

It wasn't much, Pavel decided. If Kaganov were determined, then it was even a stupid gesture. But he was not going to be responsible for any more deaths. He'd struck a bargain with Kaganov and he'd kept it. There was no need for him to go beyond what he'd already done.

'All right,' sighed Kaganov. 'You're the one who should know the man's worth.'

'Have you finished with me now?' asked Pavel. He made no effort to keep the sneer out of his voice.

'Yes,' he said. 'We're finished with you.'

The car pulled up outside his apartment and they both sat there.

'She's waiting for you,' said Kaganov, after a while. He tapped the partition and the driver got out and opened the door.

Pavel leaned across, squeezing by the other Russian.

'Pavel.'

The scientist turned. Kaganov was holding out his hand.

'Thank you,' he said. 'And goodbye.'

Pavel looked at the offered hand and then up into the man's face. Then he turned, without saying anything and walked away from the car.

The concierge smiled a greeting at him, but Pavel swept by, anxious now to get to the apartment. The lift made its usual reluctant ascent and Pavel stood, drumming his fingers against the varnished sides, impatient at its slowness.

He hesitated outside the door, preparing himself. It took several minutes. Then, quickly, he twisted the key in the lock and went in.

Valentina was standing in the middle of the room,

waiting for him. She looked nervous and he thought she had been crying.

'Hello,' she said.

'Hello.'

'I looked out of the window and saw you arrive.'

'Oh.'

They stood two feet apart, looking at each other. A wisp of hair, the grey part that she was self-conscious about, had slipped out of the band with which she had tied it back and flopped over her ear. Gently he reached out, brushing it back into place. She bent her head, trapping his hand and he kept it there.

'My darling,' he said.

She came forward and he held her, feeling her shake. He kissed her several times, waiting for the emotion to subside, then held her away from him, looking into her face.

'I missed you,' she said, softly.

'And I you … ' he said, speaking with difficulty.

'I was so worried.'

'Why?'

She humped her shoulders, finding it hard to express herself.

'You didn't come back when the show ended,' she said. 'I met Dymshits's wife in the market and she said you had stayed on, for a special reason. But no one knew what it was.'

She nodded to the corner of the room and he followed the gesture. His battered leather case stood there, still locked, near the display case showing his awards. Still junk, he thought, worthless junk.

'It came back, several days ago,' she said. Suddenly her control went and she burst into tears and he held her again, stroking her head, trying to calm her.

'I thought you had defected,' she sobbed, 'I thought you had followed Alexandre and abandoned me.'

He went on stroking her hair. 'Abandon you? You knew better than that.'

'I know. I know it was silly and I kept telling myself that, but I couldn't think of any other reason for your not coming back. I tried to find out. I asked people, but no one knew. Or wanted to know.'

'There was nothing to know ... no secret ... '

'Oh dear.' She put her hand to her mouth and flushed, embarrassed, as if he'd surprised her doing something wrong.

'What is it?'

'Oh God, how selfish of me. How can you forgive me?'

'Forgive what?'

'I'm so excited that I forgot the most important news. Georgi is back. He's got a surprise posting and he's back here in Moscow. We can be together again, like a whole family.'

She burbled on. 'And then I thought if you'd defected, then Georgi's posting would be cancelled and he'd be sent back. And we'd be arrested ... '

She started crying again.

'But I kept thinking of you. Of never seeing you again ... oh darling, I couldn't bear the thought of that ... '

She turned away, ashamed to face him.

'That's all I really thought about ... us ... just you and me. I didn't even consider the children ... am I so bad ... so selfish ... ?'

She turned back to him, nervously.

'Do you know what?'

'What?'

'I had determined ... if you had defected that is ... I'd made up my mind to kill myself. I was going to forget the children and kill myself. May God forgive me.'

He held her again and, hidden from her view, fought to control his own tears. She pushed him away, smiling.

'But now you're back. Now you're back and we're a

158

family again and Georgi is home. Tonight you'll see him.'

'Yes,' he said. 'And nothing will split us up again.'

'Promise me?' she asked.

He recognized the importance of the question to her.

'I promise,' he said. Then, remembering his arrival that morning, he added, 'I'll never go away again.'

She smiled, holding both his hands in hers. 'Forgive me, my darling,' she said, 'I'm so concerned with myself that I'm ignoring you. You must be tired. Would you like some tea?'

'Yes,' he said. 'Yes, that would be nice.'

He followed her, as he always did, into the kitchen and watched as she brewed the samovar. Occasionally she glanced up and their eyes met and they smiled, complete without conversation.

An hour later Valentina arrived home from the academy and he spent thirty minutes reading the latest reports of her prowess with the violin and then, as it was getting dark, Georgi arrived, roughened by life in the barracks, wearing his coarse uniform, slapping his father on the back, swearing occasionally to record the fact that he was an adult.

They had a celebration dinner, with Georgian wine and borsch, with mutton dumplings, and occasionally Pavel's wife cried with happiness and the children laughed at her, believing she was a little drunk.

They made love that night, unhurriedly and with great tenderness, two people treading a well-established path, and she cried again, but this time from pleasure.

He was almost asleep when she spoke and he struggled back from the edge of exhaustion, concentrating on what she was saying.

'Viktor.'

'What?'

'I know I shouldn't ask ... that because of what you do it could be none of my business ... but I was so worried ... '

'What?' he said, holding her head against his chest. 'What is it?'

'Where were you? Why didn't you come home, like the others?'

He lay quietly in the darkness, breathing deeply. So long did he take to reply that Valentina thought he had fallen asleep.

Then he said, 'I was allowed to make a visit, a special trip, to someone who helped me once ... '

Again there was a long pause. Then he added, 'I had to say goodbye to an old friend.'